***Nothing seemed certain
anymore,***

and she desperately needed to get a grip on
herself before the situation slipped completely
beyond her control.

At the end of the footpath, before they reached
the house, Nora stopped. Fletcher's Jeep was
parked a few yards away. Rain trickled down
his cheeks and made his hair cling to his head
in gleaming tendrils. His eyes were darker than
usual, cautious and thoughtful.

Softly she said, "All things considered, I think
we should skip the picnic."

"Is that what you want?"

No, it wasn't. What she wanted was to lie
in bed with him and listen to the rain lash
against the windows until the aftermath of
passion carried her into sleep. But what she
wanted now and what she would be able to
live with come morning were two entirely
different things....

Dear Reader,

Talk about starting the new year off with a bang! Look at the Intimate Moments lineup we have for you this month.

First up is Rachel Lee's newest entry in her top-selling Conard County miniseries, *A Question of Justice*. This tale of two hearts that seem too badly broken ever to mend (but of course are about to heal each other) will stay in your mind—and your heart—long after you've turned the last page.

Follow it up with Beverly Barton's *The Outcast*, a Romantic Traditions title featuring a bad-boy hero— and who doesn't love a hero who's so bad, he's just got to be good? This one comes personally recommended by #1-selling author Linda Howard, so don't miss it! In *Sam's World*, Ann Williams takes us forward into a future where love is unknown—until the heroine makes her appearance. Kathleen Creighton is a multiple winner of the Romance Writers of America's RITA Award. If you've never read her work before, start this month with *Eyewitness* and you'll know right away why she's so highly regarded by her peers—and by readers around the world. Many of you have been reading Maura Seger's Belle Haven Saga in Harlequin Historicals. Now read *The Surrender of Nora* to see what Belle Haven—and the lovers who live there—is like today. Finally there's Leann Harris's *Angel at Risk*, a story about small-town secrets and the lengths to which people will go to protect them. It's a fittingly emotional—and suspenseful—close to a month of nonstop fabulous reading.

Enjoy!

Leslie Wainger
Senior Editor and Editorial Coordinator

Please address questions and book requests to:
Silhouette Reader Service
U.S.: 3010 Walden Ave., P.O. Box 1325, Buffalo, NY 14269
Canadian: P.O. Box 609, Fort Erie, Ont. L2A 5X3

THE SURRENDER OF NORA

MAURA SEGER

Published by Silhouette Books

America's Publisher of Contemporary Romance

SILHOUETTE BOOKS

ISBN 0-373-07617-7

THE SURRENDER OF NORA

Books by Maura Seger

MAURA SEGER

and her husband, Michael, met while they were both working for the same company. Married after a whirlwind courtship that might have been taken directly from a romance novel, Maura credits her husband's patient support and good humor for helping her fulfill the lifelong dream of being a writer. Currently writing contemporaries for Silhouette and historicals for Harlequin and mainstream, she finds that writing each book is an adventure filled with fascinating people who never fail to surprise her.

Chapter 1

Dark. Thick, dense, impenetrable dark. Nora's eyes ached from it. She leaned forward, trying to see through the windshield but without much success.

Had she missed the turnoff? Should she double back, try to find it? The road was narrow, a slender black ribbon between the greater blackness of broad-trunked trees and high hedges. She couldn't see anywhere to turn around and besides, she half thought, half hoped that the turnoff was still ahead.

Too late she realized that she should have had better directions. But she had been along this road a dozen or more times, and it had seemed simple enough. South, straight out of town, the lawyer had said, on the old Route One, not the new one. Follow the signs to the beach, then take the turnoff to the left.

You'll cross the bridge and there it will be. Easy for him to say.

The night blinded her. It seemed to swallow the beams of her headlights even when she flipped them on to high. Thick clouds hid the moon and the last street lamp was several miles back.

Nora sighed and slowed the car. Her shoulders hurt. She didn't want to be here, wasn't even sure what had brought her. Beyond the obvious, of course.

Gramma was dead. She was alone on the road in the night going to a place she had never imagined would be hers yet suddenly was. If only temporarily.

Amelia's house. It rippled through her thoughts like a shimmer of gold illuminating the darkness. Ruefully she shook her head. A house, no more, and a very old one at that. Yet wreathed in family legend, the source of endless stories spun out over the generations.

For three and a half centuries, the house had stood, staring out toward the sea, its back turned on the proud town its namesake had founded. Amelia Daniels, she had been, then Amelia Marlowe, a woman of courage and grace who had defied every limitation of her world to follow her own dream.

Her descendants in all the numerous branches of the family still lived in Belle Haven, although many more had scattered across the country and around the world. As scattered as Nora herself had been until the phone call and the extraordinary news that of all Gramma's many descendants, it was Nora who would become the new mistress of Amelia's house.

What in heaven's name could Gramma have been thinking of?

The question had no answer. One aged woman's decision had shaken an entire family and turned Nora's life upside down. In time, she would right it. But for now, she would be more than content if she could just find the damn turnoff.

She slowed even further. There, up ahead, was that a break in the trees? It was and beside it, just barely visible, was the painted white rock that marked the way.

Nora sighed with relief. She steered the car onto the narrow dirt road. It was still about a quarter mile to the house but at least she knew she'd get there now. What condition it would be in was an entirely different matter.

Her headlights shone off the small bridge built in the last century after a hurricane had separated the land the house stood on from the rest of the property. On the other side, mature fruit trees, some of them centuries old, bowed gracefully beneath the rain. Nora thought of the sweet, juicy apples and pears they yielded and smiled.

Beyond the orchard lay the gardens lovingly maintained by generations of Amelia's descendants. And then, at last, the house, white clapboard with blackframed windows and twin brick chimneys, exactly as Nora remembered it. Yet not at all the same.

She sat for a moment, struck by how different the house looked empty and alone. She had never seen it like that before. On all her visits as a child and young woman, the house had seemed to overflow with love and laughter. She had known it in daylight. Now she had to rediscover it in darkness, all the life gone from it.

Cold dampness reached through the crack in the car door as Nora brought the car to a full stop. She shivered. She felt a sudden temptation to drive away. Running wasn't like her, but the house looked so dark, almost foreboding. The thought of being in it by herself sent a shiver down her back.

She could go back into town. There were several inns and even a few hotels out toward Route One. Steam showers, cable TV and room service. How could she resist?

Pride warred with the simple desire to be somewhere—anywhere—else. She hesitated, staring at the house. Was the power even still on? She couldn't envision staying there alone in the dark and the silence. It would be—

There was a sudden flicker of motion to her left, just beyond the car window. She half turned, wondering what it could be. Just as she did, the car door was wrenched open. Cold, wind and rain swept into the car. With them came the throat-gripping realization that she was not alone after all. There was a man standing beside the open door, a large, roughly dressed man smelling of dampness and night.

A man who was very angry.

"What the hell do you think you're doing?" he demanded.

Nora opened her mouth to scream but no sound came out. She froze with fear. It was the moment she and almost every other woman dreaded, the moment she'd always known might be out there waiting for her. Two self-defense courses at the gym and plenty of shared advice among female friends had made her feel at least a little prepared to deal with it.

Wrong. She couldn't move, couldn't think, could hardly breathe. Any second he was going to reach into the car and—

"Turn the damn headlights off."

Oh, God, he wanted it even darker than it was. No way, absolutely not, the headlights were her only hope. Somebody might see them and wonder who had stopped in such a remote spot.

Except no one could see her from the main road. Even if another car happened to pass on such a bad night, she'd never be noticed.

She was on her own. The only person who could help her was herself.

Nora took a deep breath. Her hands clenched so tightly on the steering wheel that the knuckles shone white. She dared a glance out of the corner of her eye.

The man was bending down, but even so she could tell that he was tall and very broad through the shoulders and chest. His hair was dark blond, probably darker than usual because of the rain. It was thick and unkempt beneath the hood of the rain jacket he wore. His face was square, the features roughly hewn. At least a day's growth of whiskers, maybe more, shadowed his jaw. But it was his eyes—icy blue and riveting—that most startled her.

Maybe she could try to reason with him. She swallowed hard and prayed her voice would hold steady. "Look, I don't know who you are, but—"

"Hamilton Fletcher, that's who, now will you *please* turn the damn headlights off?"

Please? Did assailants say that? And why was he giving her his name? Surely that was a bad idea.

"Headlights?"

"They're disturbing the owls."

Maybe she'd bumped her head. There had to be some explanation for why the world suddenly felt bent out of focus.

"Owls?"

He sighed, a deep, male sound of impatience. "Pygmy owls. They're breeding in that hollow tree over there. Your headlights are pointed straight at it."

"Oh . . ." He wasn't a mugger or a rapist or a crazy. He just had a thing for owls.

Nora flicked the headlights off. Mr. Hamilton Fletcher, all six feet plus of him, emitted a low growl of approval. "Finally. On behalf of the owls, thanks."

"You're welcome."

He straightened up and started to close the car door. "The main road is back the way you came. If you turn right, you'll be headed into town."

Nora turned the key, killing the engine. "Thanks, but I'm not lost."

Fletcher scowled at her. "What do you mean?"

"I'm where I was going. Now, if you'll excuse me, I'll just get my stuff into the house."

She shivered as the first splash of rain hit her full on. Her bag was in the back seat. Thoughts of steam showers and room service still beckoned, but she'd already been enough of a weenie. Like it or not, she was staying.

"Here?" he demanded.

"Yes, here."

"You can't."

She straightened up, bag in hand, and got her first full look at him. He really was big, well over six feet tall and with the hard, muscular look of a man who spent a great deal of time outdoors. There was nothing at all soft or yielding about him. The fear he'd provoked wasn't completely irrational, but she had it under control now. Or at least enough to look him straight in the eye and even smile slightly.

"This is my house."

He stared at her as if she was the one who was crazy. "This is Amelia's house."

Whatever Nora had expected, it wasn't to hear the name of her long-dead ancestress evoked by a backwoods owl lover with—now that she noticed—crystalline blue eyes and just the smallest dimple at the right corner of his mouth.

"How do you know about Amelia?" she asked.

He shrugged as though it was obvious. "Everybody knows. The only way you can possibly have any claim on this house is if you're—" His gaze narrowed. He looked at her hard. "If you're Liz Delaney's granddaughter."

"Bingo. I'm Nora Delaney, this is my house, and I'm going inside. You—and the owls—can do whatever you like. Good night, Mr. Fletcher."

For a moment, she thought he wasn't going to take the hint. But finally, grudgingly, he moved out of her way. She could still feel him looking at her as she fumbled with the key. When the door finally opened, she all but fell into the hall. But her relief was short-lived. The light switch nearest the door was easy enough to find. Unfortunately flicking it accomplished absolutely nothing.

"Lights are off," Fletcher said helpfully. He was still standing at the foot of the front steps, watching her. His hood had fallen back. She thought he looked almost leonine, his features bluntly chiseled and the thick mane of his hair darkened by rain.

A smug, self-satisfied lion, if ever there was one. Did he really imagine that the lack of electricity would make her turn tail and run?

Not that she didn't consider it. Cable TV and steam showers she could live without, but lights?

"There's no heat, either," he added, the very soul of helpfulness.

"I brought sweaters."

"You'll need them. Gets cold in that old house."

"I seem to remember that the fireplaces work fine." Not that she'd ever laid a fire herself, but how hard could it be? There must be matches somewhere.

"Good luck finding dry wood."

"You're just brimming over with good news, aren't you."

He scowled, that fierce, leonine glare again. "The good news is that the owls are nesting. If you disturb them—"

"If I? What about you? Maybe they don't like some big guy in blunderbuss boots sneaking up on them."

"Blunderbuss—? What's that supposed to..." He shook his head as though trying to clear it. "Never mind, I don't want to know. Good night, Miss Delaney. Try not to make too much of a racket when you leave."

She blinked once, then twice. He had gone, vanishing into the dark and the rain.

Chapter 2

Nora made her way slowly into the house. She'd had the sense to bring a flashlight, but it didn't seem to help much. The long drive coupled with the encounter with Mr. Nature had left her nerves on edge. She jumped at every looming shadow and mournful creak of the old wide-planked floors.

In the dark, everything looked different from the way she remembered. She had trouble finding her way around but eventually she found her way into the kitchen. Although modernized over the years, it retained many of its original features, including the huge walk-in fireplace that dominated one wall and—blessing of blessings—the old hand pump Gramma Liz had refused to part with.

"The power goes out too often around here," Nora remembered her saying. "When it does, we still have water. I'd just as soon keep it that way."

She'd even taught Nora to use it one long-ago summer, including the all-important lesson about the need to prime. "You've got to put a little in to get a lot out," Liz said and laughed. "Life's like that, too, child. A small effort can bring big rewards."

Maybe so, but Nora hadn't experienced that. Everything she had came from hard work, sometimes too hard, if she was honest. The assignment she'd just finished had left her worn-out. Simply getting the pump going took what little energy she had left.

Bed, she thought and found no argument within herself. Anything else she had to deal with—and there was bound to be plenty—could wait until tomorrow.

That included Mr. Nature and his romantically inclined owls. Maybe she would wake up to find she'd dreamed the whole thing. It was a nice thought to keep her company as she found sheet and blankets, and made up a bed in one of the guest rooms. By the time she finished, the cold of the old house was seeping through her layers of clothes. Deciding not to undress, Nora slipped her shoes off and crawled under the covers. She was asleep almost before her head touched the pillows.

Sunlight striking her eyes woke her. It burst through the open curtains, falling directly across the bed, demanding attention. Nora moaned and tried to burrow deeper into the covers. She felt stiff and sore, as though she'd slept in the same position all night without moving. Her throat was dry and she had the beginnings of a headache.

It wasn't the fresh start she'd hoped for, but it was all she was going to get. Reluctantly she untangled herself and sat up. For a moment, sitting on the edge of the bed, she had trouble remembering where she was. Memory crashed back, as bold as the sunlight, and she flinched.

Last night, the storm, the long drive... Mr. Nature. He probably thought she was a nut case. Certainly, she was half convinced that he was. What had he said? Something about not disturbing the owls. Yeah, right. Top of her list of things to worry about. Owls.

Coffee. Now that was a priority. She found her shoes, got into them and made her way to the bathroom. When she had finished, she went downstairs. Curtains stood open all through the house, reminding her of how much Gramma Liz had loved the peculiar light found only near the sea. Thinking about that made her feel better. She was almost smiling as she rummaged around for a coffeepot. It was there, right next to the hurricane lamps she would have to figure out before nightfall. Unless she could reach the power company and convince them to turn the electricity back on. But for how long? She had no idea how many days she'd be staying. Not very many, probably. Just enough to talk with members of the family and make a decision.

Coffee first. Everything else could wait. There was something to be said for having been an army brat. Moving around from country to country had taught her to be self-sufficient. She always carried the basic comforts needed for survival—coffee, batteries, something to read, aspirin, the essentials.

Gramma Liz had liked her coffee, too. Nora found a battered but still functional—and nonelectric—drip pot in a cupboard near the sink. She got it set up, then filled a large kettle with water to heat on the gas stove. When both the coffee and the kettle were hot, she carried them back upstairs.

The kettle barely filled the bathroom sink but she made do. Washed and in fresh clothes, she ran her fingers through her short auburn hair. The rain had stopped, the sun no longer hurt her eyes and she was feeling almost human.

Time for a look around. Downstairs, she opened the front door and stepped outside. The air was fragrant with the washed-clean smell of spring. She took a deep breath and smiled. After the previous night, almost anything would have looked good, but Amelia's house was special. Even she—nature novice that she was—knew that.

And if she did, what of Mr. Nature himself? Discounting the possibility that she really had imagined him, where had he gone to? Up a tree somewhere, studying the damn owls? Or off eating twigs and berries?

Mulling over the possibilities, she wandered into the front yard. In the distance, she could see the orchards, looking none the worse for last night's storm. If she continued around the right of the house, she would find the vegetable garden. Beyond that were flower beds interspersed with gravel paths, all lovingly tended by generations of Amelia's descendants.

Behind the house was a screen of pine trees and beyond them the sea. The salt tang of it added a pungent bite to the sweeter scents of budding trees and fertile earth.

Speaking of trees, she remembered the big old oak tree that spread its branches protectively over a corner of the yard. It was the only tree she had ever climbed, dared into it by a Nash cousin who said a kid who thought Astro Turf was a naturally occurring substance would never make it past the first branch.

Nora had, but then there had been the little problem of getting back down again. She'd made it finally, but not before convincing herself that tree climbing was vastly overrated, like most of the activities her country relatives seemed to enjoy. Give her city streets and concrete any day. At least she felt at home there.

Glancing idly at the tree, she noticed a darker spot in the rough bark of the trunk. A hole. Was that where the owls were nesting?

Curious, she walked closer to the tree and stood on tiptoe to peer into the opening. Her fingers were just brushing it when the ground gave way. Her feet flew out from under her and she landed with a thud. Before she could move or even think she felt herself being pulled along the ground, away from the tree.

Oh, God, a bear had gotten her. She should have known better than to ever come out here. Who knew how many people had died horrible deaths at the hands—paws—of marauding bears. Except . . . were there bears in this part of Connecticut? And if there were, wouldn't they have the sense to run at the first sight or sniff of a human?

But if it wasn't a bear, what was it?

The answer wasn't long in coming. She lay, disheveled and heart pounding, looking straight up into a pair of startlingly blue—and very angry—eyes.

"I'm going to ask you one more time," Fletcher said with dangerous softness, "please don't bother the owls."

Her heart was beating so hard because of the shock she'd had. Only for that reason, not for any other. It had nothing at all to do with the chiseled curve of his mouth, the sun glinting off his hair, or the overwhelming masculine presence that surrounded him. Nothing at all.

Nora got to her feet quicker than she would have thought possible. Lying down around this guy was definitely not a good idea, not if she wanted to keep any shred of reason. Slowly, trying hard not to look like she was staring at him, she looked him up and down.

She'd definitely been spending too much time with blue pin-striped manager types. Way too much. This guy was totally out of her league—big, hard, tough and unless her hormones were misfiring big time—incredibly sexy. Not even the fact that he still hadn't

shaved and that several dried leaves were tucked in
among his rumpled clothes changed that. Maybe it all
actually contributed to the raw, sensual power of the
man.

She needed another cup of coffee. Or glasses. Or
serious therapy. Whatever it took to wrench her mind
out of the decidedly lascivious curve it had just taken
and back onto the good old straight and narrow,
where it had always happily dwelt until this very instant.

First she had to get a grip on herself.

Nora cleared her throat. She took a deep breath.
She straightened her own clothes and squared her
shoulders. If she'd been able to remember it, she
would have recited the Girl Scout Pledge.

"You've been here all night?" Not exactly the most
brilliant observation, but it would have to do. She just
wished she didn't sound quite so incredulous, as if
she'd never encountered anything like him before in
her life and he had her totally buffaloed. That was true
enough, but why trot it out for him to see?

Fletcher grimaced. He ran a hand through his hair.
"I've been here three days." She stared at him in disbelief. "It's a rare chance to see pygmy owl eggs
hatching," he explained with weary patience. "I didn't
want to miss it."

Well, gee, she could understand that. Once she'd
spent two weeks tracking down a single piece of obscure information that had helped send a savings and
loan president to jail for five years. Nobody could tell

her about dogged determination. But three days? Here?

"How could you—?"

"I'm using a blind." He pointed vaguely toward what looked to Nora like a clump of leaves and branches at the back of the oak tree, around the opposite side from the opening to the owls' nest.

"You've been in there?"

He nodded. Looking rather proud of himself, he added, "I snaked a micro camera up through the xylem and right into the nest. It's working great."

"The xy-what?"

"It's like the veins and arteries of the tree. Don't worry, there's no harm done. The tree doesn't even know the camera's there."

"That would have been my guess. So you've been living in this blind for three days watching the owls?"

"Yeah, it's been great. Want to take a look?"

She'd once gone down to a sub-sub-sub-basement under an investment banking house on Wall Street and crawled through what amounted to catacombs to find where an overly ambitious stockbroker had hidden the illegal tap he was using to keep an ear on the partners' dealings.

If she could do that, she could certainly do this. Besides, the big guy really seemed to want to share the experience.

"Sure, why not?"

He looked genuinely pleased. "Great, come around this way." His brows drew together just slightly. "Oh,

I'm sorry if I was a little rough just now. You didn't
get hurt or anything, did you?''

Although the thought seemed to have just occurred
to him, he looked genuinely concerned. Nora shook
her head. "No, I'm fine."

"Good, okay now, don't make any noise."

Easy to say when he was crawling into the blind
right behind her. She could smell the pleasant, woodsy
scent clinging to his clothes and was vividly aware of
the warmth of his body so close to her own.

But she was there to see the owls. And see them she
could, much to her own astonishment, on a tiny screen
tucked away in a corner of the blind. There they were,
two of them, big-eyed, heads bobbing, fluffing their
feathers and otherwise looking busy as they roosted on
what looked like three—no, four eggs.

"They're real," she exclaimed.

Behind her, Fletcher chuckled. "Of course they are.
What did you expect?"

"I don't know. I never saw anything like this before."

"Neither have most other people. Unless pairs like
this breed successfully, there won't be much chance to
see them in the future."

"They're so small," Nora said softly. She was
struck by how vulnerable the tiny owls appeared, yet
how vigorous they were in their attentions to each
other and their eggs.

"They're tougher than they look, given half a
chance."

"What will you do when the eggs hatch?"

"Keep filming. I hope to document the entire nesting period."

"That's nice." The guys she knew hoped to make it with the blonde in the next office, buy a Maserati, retire at forty. Wanting to make movies about baby owls seemed so sweet in comparison. And so harmless.

If her instincts were anything to go by—and they usually were—thinking of Fletcher as some sort of harmless, oversized teddy bear would be a major league mistake. Just then, being so near him, so aware of his size and strength, she felt a flicker of panic. She wasn't used to being close like this. It scared her.

"I think I've seen enough," she said.

He crawled out of the blind first, making room for her to follow. Back in the sunshine, Nora brushed twigs and bits of leaves from herself. Without looking at him, she said, "Well, it's been fun, but I have to go into town to see about getting the electricity turned on and stuff like that. Don't worry, I'll stay away from the owls."

Fletcher laughed, a low, masculine sound that sent a ripple up her spine. "Again, I'm sorry if I came down kind of heavy on you. I hope you understand?"

Understand that the ground didn't feel very solid under her feet and that her heart was still thudding way too hard? Yep, she understood all that perfectly.

"No problem," she said, and beat as hasty a retreat as she could manage while still holding on to a shred of dignity. She thought she managed it pretty well, but she didn't even begin to relax until she was in her car and heading back down the road toward town.

Chapter 3

Belle Haven was the sort of place where gushy real estate agents told would-be residents that they could have not merely a life but a life-style.

At least, that was what Gramma Liz had told Nora once, when she was going on about the changes the years had brought to the town their ancestress had founded.

To be fair, it was almost as though there were two towns. One was the old, settled community that cherished its colonial and revolutionary-era buildings, held fund-raisers to publish a town history and took pride in a phone book that listed column after column of residents with the same family names.

The other was the affluent community that was home to a dozen corporate headquarters, favored by lawyers, stockbrokers and the like who moved into subdivisions of garish McMansions, ran the price up on everything and caused no end of grousing among the old-timers.

Two towns, two ways of life and too much traffic. So Nora thought as she squeezed into the last parking spot in a back lot. She was lucky to have found it. Leaving the car, she walked briskly in the direction of Main Street.

Half an hour later, she emerged from the power company office, having made her case for getting the electricity turned back on. That done, she hesitated. By rights, she should check in with her grandmother's lawyer to tell him that she was in the house and discuss what should be done next, but she dreaded doing it because she knew what the results were bound to be.

There was no way on earth that the rest of the Delaney family would simply sit by and let someone they hardly knew come into their most important legacy. They had to be organizing already to confront her. That was unavoidable, but if she could put it off just a little while longer, she would do so.

Meanwhile, it was a bright spring day and she had no tremendously urgent appointments, assignments or deadlines. For the first time in longer than she could remember, she was free to do whatever she wanted.

It wasn't fair that the first thing she thought of wanting was Fletcher. He had no right intruding into her mind like that, much less popping up so vividly in her imagination.

There he was all the same and there didn't seem to be a whole lot she could do about it. Hands thrust into her jacket pockets, she walked more quickly down the street. On the next corner, she found a bookstore.

The pleasant young woman behind the counter answered her inquiry by directing her to the fiction section. Nora browsed for a while, picking out several titles. She'd had little chance to read for pleasure in recent years. With six paperbacks tucked in the crook of her arm, she wandered into the history section.

Judging by the number of titles, it was a popular subject in Belle Haven. There were books on everything from ancient Greece to recent American presidents. In between, nestled away in a corner of a shelf, was a book about the town itself that caught Nora's eye.

She took it down and glanced at the title. *The Women of Belle Haven.* Adding it to her selections, she went back to the counter to pay.

"You'll enjoy this," the young woman said as she rang up the history book. "It's pretty lively."

"Is it really?" Nora couldn't remember reading a lot of lively history. At best, she hoped for interesting.

"You bet," the young woman said. "The author's Patrick Delaney. He lives here in town. His family's related to the original founders." Her eyes twinkled. "He got hold of some private family records and decided to make them public for the first time." She laughed. "It caused a big to-do, let me tell you. For a while, it was all anyone talked about."

"When was this?" Nora asked. A distant memory was trying to surface. Something she could remember hearing about a while back but couldn't quite place.

"Going on ten years ago, I think. Anyway, the book's sold steadily ever since. We always keep at least a few copies in stock."

"I'll read it first then," Nora said, taking her bag. "Thanks."

"Sure thing."

Back out on the sidewalk, Nora stood for a moment looking around. She was tempted to find a place to sit down and at least take a peek through Patrick Delaney's book, but she had other things to do first.

To begin with she needed to pick up some food and other supplies. Dodging traffic, she found the supermarket she had noticed on the other side of the street. At this hour of the morning, it was almost empty. Wheeling her cart up and down the aisles, she tried to decide how long she was likely to be in Belle Haven.

If she was strictly practical, she'd stay just long enough to meet with the lawyers and decide what to do about the house. But if that was her only concern, she really hadn't even needed to make the trip. Something else had drawn her, a sense of respect and love for her grandmother, who had left her such an unexpected and astonishing legacy. Above all, she needed to understand why Elizabeth Delaney had done it.

She brought her groceries to the car and returned the cart. Walking back toward the parking lot, Nora was trying to decide what to do next when she spied a familiar face coming toward her. At least, the face was distantly familiar. She might be mistaken but she suspected she was about to run smack into one of her relatives. Could she slip by unrecognized? Or should she take the bull by the horns, as it were, and confront the situation head on?

The decision was made for her when the well-dressed, middle-aged woman suddenly stopped. Her mouth tightened. "It's you," she said accusingly. "Peter's child."

Nora nodded. She really hadn't wanted this to happen, not right now anyway. But she wasn't about to run from it. "Yes," she said quietly. "Peter Delaney's my father. I'm Nora."

"I know who you are," the woman said. "I would have known you anywhere even though we scarcely see you." She grimaced slightly. "Your father wasn't exactly regular in his visits."

Patiently Nora replied. "He was in the army. We moved around a lot. You're Charlotte Delaney, aren't you?"

"That's right. We're cousins of some sort or another, although I couldn't tell you exactly how off the top of my head. How long have you been in town?"

"I got here last night."

"And you're staying . . . ?"

Bull by the horns, Nora reminded herself. "At the house." There was no need to say which house. Charlotte Delaney knew instantly.

Her mouth tightened further. "I see. Don't you think that's taking quite a bit on yourself?"

"Not really. After all, Grandmother did leave the house to me."

"Yes, I know. We all know. Frankly it's been just about all we've talked about since Elizabeth passed on. Her decision was extraordinary. We barely knew who you were and suddenly there you are, in possession of a legacy that rightly belongs to—"

"To who?" Nora demanded softly. She wasn't angry; Charlotte Delaney's feelings were perfectly natural. But neither was she about to apologize for being her grandmother's heir. Unexpected though it was, Elizabeth had been entirely within her rights to leave the house to anyone she chose.

Charlotte Delaney didn't agree. Staring down her aquiline nose, she said bluntly, "The house should have gone to other members of the family. We were prepared to hold it jointly. There has been discussion for several years now of turning it into a museum. Certainly it is far too important to be left to a young woman with only the most tenuous connection to the family."

"I wouldn't call my connection exactly tenuous. Elizabeth Delaney was my grandmother."

"She had nine other grandchildren besides you. Have you thought of that? Your father was one of four children, the only one who chose to make a life for himself entirely away from Belle Haven."

"He always stayed in touch with Grandmother wherever we happened to be. But that's really beside the point. Elizabeth was the sole owner of Amelia's house and she had the sole right to decide what would happen to it. You may not like that, but it is the fact.''

''I—or more correctly we—don't have to like it or live with it. You might as well know that we are prepared to contend that in the final days of her life, Elizabeth Delaney was not in full possession of her faculties.''

''I visited Grandmother two weeks before she died and I certainly didn't see any sign that her mind had gone. On the contrary, she was completely lucid and very aware of everything.''

''Did she tell you then that she was leaving you the house?''

''No,'' Nora admitted. ''She didn't mention it.''

Charlotte nodded vigorously. ''Because she changed her will right after your visit. I'd like to know what sort of influence you brought to bear to make her do it.''

''Influence?'' Nora was shocked. Did anyone seriously believe that she had conspired somehow to get Elizabeth to leave her the house? The very suggestion was ludicrous.

''Influence,'' Charlotte repeated. ''You must have done something. Why else would she have made such an insane decision? Believe me, we won't rest until we find out what happened and undo it.''

Nora swallowed an angry reply. With strict self-control, she said, ''Do whatever you like, Mrs. Delaney, but keep in mind if there's one thing I learned from my father, it was never to let anyone walk over me. If you challenge Grandmother's will, you'll have a fight on your hands. I promise you that.''

Charlotte's face reddened. She looked as though she wanted to lash back but was momentarily at a loss for words. With a final, contemptuous glance, she stalked off.

Nora continued on to the parking lot. She got into her car and sat for a moment, staring sightlessly through the windshield. Distantly she noticed that her hands on the steering wheel were rock steady. She could be proud of that, especially considering the turmoil whirling inside her.

With a weary sigh, she started the car and headed back toward Amelia's house.

Chapter 4

Nora unloaded the groceries in the kitchen and put them away. It was cold in the old house. The electricity hadn't come back on yet; she had to trust it would soon.

Meanwhile, she put on an extra sweater and made a pot of coffee. It helped a little, but the encounter with Charlotte had left her feeling bruised inside. She thought about reading—Patrick Delaney's book still beckoned—but when she tried, she couldn't seem to concentrate.

Thoughts and questions about Elizabeth kept darting through her mind. Here, in the house where her grandmother had lived for so many years, her presence was inescapable. Nora found herself wandering from room to room, thinking about things her grand-mother had said and done.

She had always considered Elizabeth to be an intelligent, forthright woman of strength and courage. Nothing she'd seen at the end had changed that. Now, remembering Charlotte's angry words, she couldn't help but wonder. Was Elizabeth's decision to leave the house to her no more than a surprising choice or was it the product of a damaged mind?

It hurt to even think that her grandmother might have suffered a loss of reason in her final days, but the possibility couldn't be dismissed entirely. At least, not without some evidence to the contrary.

She was staring out the window, sipping her coffee, when she noticed the blind. It was still there so she supposed Fletcher was, too. He'd made himself at home practically on Gramma Liz's doorstep. Surely that must mean he'd known her.

The impulse to march outside and ask him was almost irresistible, but Nora restrained herself. It took very little imagination to guess how he'd react. Like it or not, she would have to wait until he surfaced for air or whatever.

In the meantime, she had work to do. She was lucky that her current assignment allowed her to work off site. Combing through reams of computerized data about financial transactions wasn't her idea of a good time, but it could pay off big.

She set up her notebook computer on the kitchen table, refilled her coffee cup and got busy. As she began to study a file, Nora smiled. For over three and a half centuries, women of her family had baked bread, washed clothes, cooked meals, stitched wounds and even had babies in this kitchen. They'd brewed herbal medicines, planned gardens, counseled neighbors and debated the great issues of their day.

The old whitewashed walls had seen no end of activity, but she was willing to bet this was the very first time anyone had ever switched on a computer, activated a cellular modem and prepared to investigate the arcane doings of a major international corporation. Not even Amelia's house was immune from the huge changes happening everywhere. Here, too, the twenty-first century was just around the corner.

Had Elizabeth been thinking of that when she named Nora her heir?

Neat columns of numbers spread out in front of her, but Nora couldn't concentrate. The electricity came back on suddenly, provoking a small cheer from her. Lights lit up all around the kitchen and there was a soft hum as the pump started up in the basement. She plugged in the computer's power pack to conserve its battery but work still remained elusive. Try though she did, thoughts of her grandmother kept intruding. She was struggling to make sense of what she was looking at—without any success—when there was a knock at the kitchen door.

Glad of the interruption, Nora jumped up. She opened the door without even thinking to ask who was on the other side, proof all by itself that she wasn't entirely herself. No sensible city dweller would ever take such a chance.

"Sorry to bother you," Fletcher said. He looked bigger, more disheveled and even more male than before. His beard was thicker than ever. There were more leaves and twigs stuck to his clothes. He carried with him the scent of fresh air, fertile earth and nights spent under a starlit sky.

"It's no bother," she murmured and stood aside to let him in.

His attention was drawn to the computer on the table. "You're working."

"Not very well. Actually I was hoping to have a chance to talk with you. Would you like some coffee?"

It really wasn't fair that he could smile like that, a sudden, flashing change in his expression that made her chest feel tight.

"I'd love some," he said. "I brought several thermoses along, but they were empty a couple of days ago."

"Haven't you been able to cook?"

"Not really. A fire would—"

"Disturb the owls."

He grinned a little sheepishly. "That's right."

Nora went over to the stove and poured him a large mug from the pot. As she handed it to him, she asked, "Any sign of the eggs hatching?"

He took a long, appreciative swallow and shook his head. "Not so far. I really thought they would by now but we don't know all that much about pygmy owl breeding habits. That's the whole point of doing this."

"I guess, but it must be kind of tough on you."

"I'm getting a lot of reading done, but there are still problems. That's what I wanted to talk with you about." He hesitated before continuing. "I really didn't expect this to take so long. I brought fresh clothes with me, but I'd just about kill for a shower. My cabin's about five miles down the beach. If I head back there, I may miss the eggs starting to hatch. I know that probably doesn't sound like much but after waiting this long—"

"You can take a shower here," Nora said. She was proud of the way she said it, calmly, even casually, as though the thought of him standing naked with water sluicing off his body had no effect on her at all.

"That's great," he said. "I really appreciate this. Just one other thing, would you mind..." He hesitated.

"What?"

"No, forget it. The shower's terrific. Thanks a lot. I won't be long."

"Take as long as you want. I'll go watch the eggs."

He looked at her as though she were the most marvelous creature he'd ever seen. Nora sighed, wondering how many women would have crawled over the coals of hell for a look like that from a man like Fletcher. No doubt about it, life wasn't fair. Heck, there were times when it was flat-out nuts.

She should be working. The bright little screen of the computer beckoned cheerfully. That was where she belonged and what she knew. Not this insides-melting, cheeks flushed, brain-shutting-down excitement that seemed to seize her whenever she got within a hundred feet of Hamilton Fletcher.

Nuts. But at least it got her out of the house while he showered.

"First sign of anything happening, I'll come and get you."

"Thanks a lot."

Nora didn't hang around to hear or see anything else. She grabbed her jacket off the peg by the door and went outside. It was getting on for late afternoon. The air had a golden hue and quiet pressed in all around her. She couldn't remember the last time she'd been somewhere so peaceful. Walking across the yard to the old oak tree, it was possible to forget the year, even the century. Time itself seemed to blend together.

Going carefully, she crawled into the blind. The camera screen showed the owls still sitting almost exactly as she had seen them before. They blinked in her direction as though in welcome.

With a sigh, she settled down to wait. At this distance from the house, it was absolutely impossible to hear the shower. But in her imagination she did. Saw, as well, all too clearly Fletcher reaching for the soap, rubbing it between his large hands, spreading the foam over his chest—

Sweet heaven, what was happening to her? She hadn't been this giddy when she was fifteen years old. Moving every year or two hadn't exactly encouraged adolescent fantasies. She'd been a loner, proud and self-sufficient, and she'd done just fine. Why the sudden change?

Maybe it was the air around Amelia's house or the way the sunlight filtered through the tree branches. Or perhaps it had more to do with the house itself and the sense she had of belonging there in a way she had never experienced before.

But that was crazy. Her stay here was strictly temporary. She had a life, a career, friends, colleagues, everything she could want. She would have to be out of her mind to even consider—

What was that? A tiny sound interrupted her train of thought. Instinctively she stared at the camera. The owls were flapping their wings as though something had happened to excite them. Nora peered closer. Was that a faint, hairline crack appearing on one of the eggs?

Moments passed before she realized her eyes were playing tricks. The owls must be as bored as she was. Absolutely nothing was happening with the eggs.

With a sigh, she settled back down to wait. Fifteen minutes or so later, she heard movement in front of the blind. Nora crawled back out. She straightened up, dusting off her hands, and stared into the face of a man she recognized right enough but who still looked startlingly different.

To begin with, he had shaved. The thick growth of beard that had concealed the lower half of his face was gone, revealing smooth, burnished skin and chiseled features. He'd washed and brushed his hair so that it glinted in the sunlight. There were no twigs or leaves attached to his clothes. He wore a clean plaid shirt and khakis that still had the creases in them. He could have stepped out of the kind of magazine that portrayed impossibly handsome men posed against backdrops of trout streams and other natural stuff. But he was here, in her yard, right in front of her.

Nora took a deep breath and ignored the flutter right in the middle of her stomach. "Hi." Maybe it wasn't the most scintillating thing to say, but it was all she could think of just then.

"Hi. Anything happening?"

Happening? Well, yeah, but probably not the way he meant. "The owls were fluttering around a few minutes ago, but nothing seemed to come of it."

"I'll take a look." He knelt down and eased his way into the blind. Nora tried really hard not to stare, but she couldn't help noticing how nicely the khakis fit him. She was looking up at the sky, watching the clouds, when he reemerged.

"You're right, nothing's changed."

"Sorry."

"That's okay. They've got to hatch eventually. At least I got cleaned up. Thanks."

"No problem. Well, I guess I'd better be getting back."

"I noticed the computer. What kind of work do you do?"

Nora sighed inwardly. She hated explaining what she did for a living. Invariably she got the same reaction—glazed eyes and incomprehension. Still, she might as well get it over with. "I'm a forensic accountant. I investigate companies' accounting practices to make sure they're in line with legal requirements."

Fletcher blinked once, then twice. For just a second, he looked a little like the owls. "Sounds interesting."

Nora laughed. "No, it doesn't. Most people think the work I do is as dry as the desert but in fact, it has its moments."

"Like when?"

"Like when I come across a guy who thinks the law doesn't apply to him. It's always a big surprise when he discovers that it actually does."

"That's kind of reassuring. Who do you work for, the government?"

Nora shook her head. "I'm with an independent auditing firm. The partners don't much like the idea of signing off on a company, telling investors that it's okay, only to find out a year or two down the line that the books were cooked. They prefer for me to discover that going in."

"And you do?"

"From time to time. Most of the companies I check out are perfectly reputable, but every once in a while, I come up against a bad one."

Fletcher frowned. "What happens then?"

Nora smiled. "Then my job gets really interesting."

"It sounds as though it could get dangerous, too."

"Not so far. Anyway, I don't worry about it." She hesitated before shifting gears. "Look, I know you want to get back to the eggs, but do you mind if I just ask you a question?''

"Shoot.''

"How well did you know my grandmother?''

"Pretty well, I'd say. I met her six years ago when I moved out here. There have been times when I've been away—sometimes for months at a stretch—but when I've been around I'd see her maybe every other week or so, sometimes more. She was a nice lady.''

Nora took a deep breath. Quietly she asked, "Did you see much of her toward the end?''

Fletcher nodded. He looked at her closely. "I stopped by regularly. Why?''

"I just wondered. I saw her myself two weeks before she died. She was obviously fading, but we talked about lots of things, laughed, actually had a good time together. I don't think I let myself realize she would go so soon after that.''

Fletcher was silent for a moment. Softly he asked, "What's this all about, Nora? Your grandmother loved your visits and the phone calls, letters, all the things you sent. You stayed in close touch with her and she appreciated it.''

"I know . . . it's just that . . .''

"That what?''

Nora took a deep breath. She didn't want to ask, but she had to know. "Do you think toward the end her mind was affected?''

He looked startled. "Liz's? No way. Her body failed, but her mind certainly never did.'' His gaze narrowed. "Where did you get that idea?''

"It doesn't matter. I—"

"Yeah, it does matter. If someone's suggesting that Liz Delaney wasn't in full possession of her faculties at the time of her death, that's baloney. She was one of the sharpest people I ever met."

Nora smiled faintly. What he'd said reassured her, but she still had doubts. "Then maybe you can explain why she did what she did."

"You mean leaving the house to you?"

"That's right. Apparently there are people in the family who think she must have been coerced or otherwise unduly influenced."

Fletcher laughed. "Let me guess, you ran into Charlotte Delaney."

"How did you know?"

"Everybody knows Charlotte. Hell, she's on just about every town committee, board, council, whatever. Don't get me wrong, she's done some real good, but she doesn't tend to see other people's points of view."

"She sure doesn't see mine," Nora admitted. "Or Gramma's, for that matter."

"If Charlotte's suggesting that Liz didn't know what she was doing when she left the house to you, she's barking up the wrong tree."

Nora looked at him gratefully. "I hope so. Whatever comes of it, I can't bear the thought of Gramma doing this for any reason except that she believed it was best."

"I'm sure that's exactly what she did believe.

There's really only one thing you ought to be wondering about.''

''What's that?''

His eyes held hers. Softly, on the fragrant air, he said, ''Was she right?''

Nora had no answer.

Chapter 5

Halfway through a file labeled: Kincaid Industries International Contracts, first quarter, Nora shivered. The power might be back but that didn't seem to be doing the old house's heating system any good. As the sun slanted behind the trees, the temperature was falling fast.

She already had one sweater on. It didn't feel as though another would help much. Last night, she'd thought about making a fire, but had been too tired to do anything about it. Now she decided to try.

How hard could it be? A quick check around the house turned up plenty of wood. She had her choice of fireplaces. The one in the kitchen looked a little too big to tackle, but the front parlor fireplace looked just right.

She moved her computer onto a small table in the parlor, then set to work laying a fire. Besides the wood, there was kindling, old newspapers and even matches. She put some of each in the fireplace but that didn't really look like enough, so she added more. Satisfied, and just a little pleased with herself, she struck a match and tossed it in.

Nothing happened. Peering into the fireplace, she found the match—out.

Fine, she'd try again, but this time she'd do it right. If one match didn't work, maybe several would. Lighting matches in quick succession, she held the small flames to the newspapers until the edges caught and began to smoke. By the time she was done, all the paper was burning and the small bits of kindling were beginning to catch.

She stood up, wiped her hands off and turned to go back to work. Just then, a wisp of smoke went past her. That was odd. Wasn't it supposed to go up the chimney?

Nora turned and gasped. Smoke was pouring out of the fireplace into the room. She looked around frantically for something, anything, to put the fire out, but there was nothing. She ran for the kitchen, intending to get a bucket of water, but the smoke was thickening so quickly that she doubled over, coughing.

By the time she'd filled the bucket, smoke was billowing through the downstairs. Nora couldn't even see the fireplace. She stumbled across the parlor, one hand clutching the bucket and the other over her nose and mouth. Her eyes burned. She could barely breath. All she could think of was what would happen if she didn't manage to put the fire out.

Amelia's house had survived more than three and a half centuries. There was a terrible irony in the thought that she, the prodigal granddaughter, might be the person who destroyed it.

Desperately she struggled to find her way, but the smoke was everywhere, obscuring her vision and filling her lungs. Remembering what she'd been told long ago in a fire safety class in grade school, she dropped to the floor and tried pushing the bucket in front of her.

That was a little better but not much. She still could hardly see or breathe. Her heart rammed against her ribs. She was suddenly, terrifyingly afraid that she might lose consciousness and be trapped there in the suffocating smoke.

"What the hell—?" The deep voice, perplexed and annoyed, cut through the panic at the edge of Nora's mind. She stiffened and instinctively tried to straighten up, only to be pushed back down onto the floor.

"Stay there," Fletcher ordered. He made a sound of pure male exasperation and left her. A moment later, she heard the grating noise of metal on stone. Almost at once, a rush of clear air filled the room as the smoke began to ease.

"It's called a flue," Fletcher said as he put a hand under Nora's elbow and lifted her. "You open it *before* you start the fire. That way, the smoke goes up the chimney." As an afterthought, he added, "That's the tall thing sticking out of the top of the house."

Nora flushed. She was enormously relieved that the crisis was over but she didn't need to be reminded of how inept she'd been. "I know what a chimney is," she murmured.

He looked down at her from the considerable—and blatantly unfair—advantage nature had given him. His expression softened a little, but he still looked like an exasperated, irate lion disturbed from his slumber. "What about the rest?"

She lifted her shoulders self-consciously. "I guess you could say I'm not much of a Girl Scout."

Fletcher laughed. "Why am I relieved by that?"

"I haven't the faintest idea. Look, I really appreciate your help. Obviously I didn't know what I was doing. I'm still worried I may have damaged the house."

"I doubt it. This old place has been through a lot worse."

Nora wanted to believe him, but her concern didn't lessen. He must have seen that because he said more gently, "Let's get all the windows opened. You don't want the smoke to sink into the furniture."

Half an hour later, the downstairs was so cold that Nora stood with her arms wrapped around herself, shivering. But the smoke was gone and no permanent harm seemed to have been done.

There was even a fire burning cheerfully in the parlor. "That should do it," Fletcher said as he began closing the windows again. Nora helped him. By the time they finished, dusk was settling over the house.

"I'm going to make some tea," Nora said. She started to ask if he'd like some but caught herself. "You have to get back to the owls."

Fletcher hesitated. He gave her a long, steady look that made her toes curl and smiled. "Actually I'm beginning to suspect they know I'm there."

"Would that make a difference?"

"Depends. Owls can be ornery."

"If you say so." His eyes really were the most startling shade of blue. "I'll make that tea."

He followed her into the kitchen. It was a large room, but Fletcher seemed to make it shrink. Nora snuck a quick glance at him as she ran water into the kettle. Seated at the wooden table with his long legs stretched out in front of him, he looked perfectly at home.

"I guess you've always lived out in the country?" she asked, putting the kettle on the stove.

"You think so?"

"Well, you do seem to belong in a place like this and it's a fair bet you know how to manage a lot better than I do."

"No offense, but I know folks who have never been farther west than Fifth Avenue who would have known to open that flue."

"You're kidding?"

"No, honest, but like I said, no offense meant."

"None taken, but I was referring to your knowing people from New York City. Do you really?"

"Hard not to, considering that's where I was born and raised."

"No."

"Absolutely. Want to hear my Brooklyn accent?"

"I'll pass, thanks. You're serious, you grew up in New York?"

Fletcher nodded. "Till I was eighteen. Then I went off to college and grad school, bummed around some and ended up here."

"Why Belle Haven?"

"Family ties. A couple of ancestors of mine were around when the place was founded."

"Really? I didn't know that."

He smiled faintly. "I can see how you wouldn't. Apparently one of the settler's daughters got a little too friendly with the local chief's son."

"Sounds like a paperback romance."

"Not really. The outcome was tragic. She was almost killed by an enraged Puritan minister, the Indians rebelled and the chief's son died. But her child lived and for better or worse, Fletchers have been here ever since."

Nora spooned tea into the caddie. She set brightly flowered mugs on the table. This wasn't fussing. She was simply doing what she would do for herself with the only difference that it was for two. Which reminded her, it was getting on for dinner. When she was working, she often forgot to eat or just ate a sandwich at the computer. But she'd picked up a roasted chicken at the deli counter along with a couple of salads.

"I can fix us a quick bite to eat, if you'd like," she said.

For just a moment, he had the starved look of a man who had been living on beef jerky and dried soup, but he controlled himself admirably. "I wouldn't want you to go to any trouble."

"Don't worry, I wouldn't know how. Cooking got left out of my repertoire. However, you can set me down in any city on earth and I can locate a decent take-out place in under five minutes."

He laughed. "Now there's a skill to be proud of, but what happens when you aren't in a city?"

"Then I'm here. Except for visits to Gramma Liz, my life has pretty well been all cities."

"That's too bad. There's a lot to the world elsewhere."

"If you say so. Chicken okay?"

"From a chicken bush?"

"Of course, although to tell you the truth, I always wondered how they managed to grow the packages wrapped in plastic."

"Just one more miracle of nature," Fletcher said and grinned. "I'll take a quick look at the owls and be right back."

"Deal."

Nora's heart beat a little quicker, but she told herself that was from the unaccustomed exertion of putting dinner on the table for two. It had nothing to do with the fact that she couldn't remember the last time she'd had a purely social dinner with a man. Breakfast, lunch and dinner—when not taken on the run—tended to be business occasions. For several years, she'd been meaning to get a life beyond work. She just hadn't gotten around to it yet.

What was it Gramma Liz had said the last time Nora saw her? "Life's too short, child. Not a day of it should be wasted."

Just looking around the old house made it clear that Elizabeth Delaney had lived her life to the fullest. There were shelves of books she had read and cherished, the piano she'd played, paintings she'd done and the garden she had lovingly cultivated. All that and she'd raised four children, followed a genuine vocation in herbal medicine, and been a pillar of her community.

Nora couldn't help but envy her just a little. She had always been much narrower in focus, concentrating on her career to the exclusion of just about everything else. It had never occurred to her that there was anything wrong with that, until now.

The chicken was warming in the oven and the salads had been transferred to serving bowls when she realized Fletcher hadn't come back. Puzzled, she was about to stick her head out the door when it was yanked open.

"Come on," Fletcher said, "you've got to see this." He grabbed her hand and headed back toward the blind.

Chapter 6

One egg had hatched and eager peeps were coming from the others before Nora remembered she'd left the chicken in the oven. A frantic scramble to the house meant she almost missed the second egg opening, but she was back and watching when the tiny owl pecked its way into the world, all huge eyes and ruffled feathers.

"They're amazing," she said softly. The greenish light of the video monitor filling the blind couldn't detract from the beauty of what she was witnessing. No matter how many times life came into the world in all its various forms, each occurrence was the reminder of a miracle.

"No wonder you were willing to be so patient," Nora murmured.

Fletcher nodded. "I'm not usually, but this is really something special." He cast her a quick sidelong glance. "I'm glad you got to see it."

"So am I."

They were silent for a long time after that, both caught up in the drama unfolding before them. The hatchlings were so small, yet so valiant, so determined, so touching. Nora actually felt tears in her eyes when the adult owls began to gently groom the damp, new-fledged feathers with their beaks. Soon the baby owls were dry and fluffy. They began opening and closing their beaks with obvious intent.

"They're hungry," Nora said. She thought of the chicken sitting on the kitchen counter. "Can we feed them?"

Fletcher shook his head. "I know it seems like you'd be helping, but there's too much of a risk of their becoming dependent on humans. They're better off taking care of themselves."

Even as he spoke, one of the owls roused itself and took several quick prancing steps toward the tree hole. It stood for a moment, bobbing on the edge, before suddenly taking off on a whisper of wings.

"Where did it go?" Nora asked.

"To hunt."

"I thought they only did that at night."

"Dusk is good enough. Besides, the kids are hungry. Why hang around listening to them complain when you can go do something about it?"

She shook her head, staring at the screen where the mother owl—or was it the father? she shouldn't be sexist about this—was busy again grooming the chicks. It looked less like a necessity now and more like a ploy for keeping them distracted until dinner arrived.

"It's hard to believe such little things can actually go out and kill something."

"If you were a field mouse, you'd see it differently. Owls of any kind are among the most accomplished hunters in the animal kingdom. Besides mice, they'll go after small snakes, rabbits, other birds, pretty much anything that isn't significantly bigger than them."

"Rabbits—as in bunnies?"

He shrugged, but didn't look especially contrite. "Sorry, that's how it is. Nature's pretty ruthless."

"I've always suspected as much. Give me concrete and asphalt any day."

"You mean where the predators are your own size and probably better armed? At least most animals only hunt to eat. The same can't be said for humans."

"Is that why you left? Too much human company?"

"I guess so. I've always felt more at home in places like this."

Nora laughed. "I can understand that. My first apartment in New York was about the same size as this place."

He shook his head in bemusement. "How could you stand that?"

"I wasn't home much. It was just somewhere to store clothes and sleep."

"And now?" He was looking at her closely, his eyes dark and unreadable. Small as it was, the blind seemed to shrink suddenly. She could feel the heat of his body, smell the crisp, clean scent of him. There was a thrumming in her ears, blood rushing, her heart murmuring of things she didn't want to hear.

"The apartment's bigger and the neighborhood's a little fancier, but I guess I still feel the same."

"Hang your hat and collect your mail?"

How did he manage to make her so self-conscious, so painfully aware of issues in her life that she had done a darn good job of avoiding all these years? He was a stranger, yet he wasn't. Some hidden part of her seemed to recognize him in a way she could neither understand nor deny.

Yet to be fair, maybe it wasn't just Fletcher. Maybe it was being here, in the shadow of Amelia's house, so close to all the hopes and dreams of the women who had gone before her. She had been a loner all her life but here, in this place, her solitude was ebbing. Like it or not, she felt caught up in forces vastly larger than herself.

"I'll understand if you want to skip dinner," she said.

His gaze was long and level, as though he was weighing something in his own mind. Slowly his eyes lightened. A smile played around the corners of his finely chiseled mouth.

"I think we can trust the owls on their own for a while. Besides, the camera will pick up anything that happens."

"If you're sure..."

Her own doubt was making itself all too evident. Of all the men she had ever met, she couldn't think of one who radiated the raw, almost primitive masculinity that was Fletcher's. Yet there was nothing rough or cruel about him. On the contrary, she sensed a quiet strength and confidence that was all but irresistible.

All but. She was a grown woman, independent and self-sufficient. Surely she could stand a few hours in Hamilton Fletcher's company without making a fool of herself? Besides, he wasn't her type. As soon as she got this business with the house sorted out, she'd be back where she belonged, back to the concrete and the asphalt where the men wore pinstripe, not denim, and worried about their careers, not newborn owls.

Not like this man of the forest and the night who filled her with confusion and what felt perilously like longing.

She should never have asked him to dine, but there was no going back now. Like it or not, she was bound on a course she hadn't set. The sensation was unsettling, to say the least, like lightning come without warning to a peaceful sky.

"Dinner," she said before she could say something else entirely. The blind was too small, she couldn't breathe. Quickly she scrambled out and stood for a moment, taking in lungfuls of air.

Night had fallen while they were watching the hatchlings. A pale moon sailed high above. By its light, she saw Amelia's house, widows golden against the darkness, smoke curling from the chimney, warm and welcoming, as it had been for so many others through so many years.

The sight calmed her. Head high, step steady, she walked toward the house. Behind her, silvered in moonlight, an owl called.

He set the table. Without being asked, he found the brightly painted plates, the forks and knives, the glasses and set them out neatly on woven place mats. He even remembered the salt and pepper.

"You cooked," he said when Nora thanked him.

"Not exactly. The nice man at the deli should really get the credit."

Fletcher laughed, that deep, rich sound that sent a tremor straight down her spine. He held out Nora's chair. "Is it true that in some apartments in New York, there's no oven anymore, just a microwave?"

She sat down and spread her napkin carefully. The simplest action seemed to require more attention than usual, so distracting was he.

"That's what I've heard," she said. "Of course, what you really want is for the take-out to get delivered fast enough not to need warming up."

Fletcher took his seat across from her. He poured wine for them both. "What's the hurry?"

Nora passed the chicken. She'd sliced it into more or less tidy pieces and arranged it neatly on a plate. Just as she would have done for herself—once or twice in her life. Pretending great interest in a piece of white meat, she said, "We live in an instant gratification society. People want their needs fulfilled immediately so they can get on to the next thing.''

''And the next and the next. Everything comes quickly and goes just as fast. Nothing has any real value.''

He smiled as he spoke, not just with that chiseled mouth, but with his eyes as well. Small lines shone at the far corners, the fine tracings of wind and sun, and his own good humor.

''You're not that cynical,'' she protested, and handed him the salad.

''Not at the moment,'' he agreed and helped himself.

''Do you mind if I ask what you do when you aren't filming owls?''

''Mostly landscape design. I'm actually a botanist, but my major interest is how the different elements of the biosphere interact. Designing environments gives me a good opportunity to observe cause-and-effect relationships.''

Oh, great. Looks, raw male energy *and* a brain. Did anyone still think life was fair?

''Sounds fascinating,'' Nora said. ''More chicken?''

The conversation moved on to other things. Fletcher knew a great deal about the house. With Nora's encouragement, he explained which parts had been built first and how it had been added on to over the generations. He described the hurricane that had severed Daniels' Neck from the mainland and the building of the bridge to reconnect it.

"Even before that happened," he said, "this area was becoming a refuge for local wildlife. It still is. There are very few pieces of land in this part of the country that are so unspoiled, especially along the coast."

"I guess that's why the owls are here?"

"Them and a whole lot more. You really ought to take a closer look around."

"Truth be told, I'm not sure I'd know what I was looking at."

His smile deepened. He reached for the wine and refilled both their glasses. "No problem. Consider me your friendly local guide. How about a picnic tomorrow?"

"Uh . . . what about the owls?"

"Actually I wasn't planning to bring them along."

"No, I mean don't you have to . . . watch them or something?"

"Not all the time. After all, I'm here, aren't I?"

He was that. Right there in front of her, all piercing blue eyes and smile. Friendly? She supposed he was, also dangerous, if only to her peace of mind.

But then peace could be highly overrated. She'd inherited Daniels' Neck. The least she could do was get to know it better.

And Fletcher, too.

"All right," she said and lifted the wineglass to her lips.

Chapter 7

The alarm woke Nora at 6:00 a.m. She fumbled for it, missing several times before managing to find the Off switch. Groaning, she fought the urge to go back to sleep. The bed was warm, the sky was just beginning to lighten and she felt as though she'd barely closed her eyes. In a sense that was true. She had lain awake far too long, staring at the ceiling, seeing images of Fletcher and those damn owls.

What was happening to her? She was such a sane, self-sufficient person. Or at least she had been. Here in this old house, filled with murmurings of the wind and sea—and perhaps more—she felt as though she was losing herself.

Enough of that. It was morning; she had things to do. Swinging her legs over the side of the bed, she got up and marched herself into the bathroom before she could change her mind. Showered and dressed in jeans and a soft golden turtleneck sweater, she went downstairs.

Normally she wasn't much of a breakfast eater, but this morning she made an exception. Half a container of blueberry yogurt and two slices of toast later, she was ready to go to work.

Kincaid Industries was a fascinating assignment. On the surface, it appeared to be a successful, international company involved in real estate investments. But the deeper Nora looked, the more she realized that there were layers upon layers of activity, all leading off into a maze of subsidiary companies, outside boards of directors, offshore holdings and so on.

None of that was unheard of in the real estate business, but all of it taken together made her more cautious than she might ordinarily have been. Why exactly was Kincaid Industries so complex? Had it merely developed that way because of its rapid growth or was there another reason?

She intended to find out, but as she resumed reviewing files on the computer in the kitchen, her thoughts kept wandering. Fletcher had said he'd come by around lunchtime. He was determined to show her Daniels' Neck in all its glory. Okay, fine, it wouldn't do her any harm to get out for a while, maybe it would even do her some good.

But she would keep it short and make it clear that she had to get back to work. She absolutely would not let herself be distracted by six feet plus of rampant

masculinity and a nature that was by turns discon-
certingly gentle and alarmingly compelling.

Sooner or later, she had to make a decision about
what to do with Amelia's house. If she was going to
choose correctly, it made sense to get as much information as possible. Fletcher could help her with that.
In a sense, he was research, something she was very
good at.

She hit a few more keys and grinned. Research.
Right. If she went on like this, she wouldn't need fingers to type. Her nose would be long enough to do it.

Okay, a little picnic, a little tour, a little rapid
heartbeat. She'd be fine. He was a nice man under all
those muscles and burnished skin, and she was a sensible woman. Heaven knew she was sensible. Steady,
reliable, predictable. Boring.

Whoa, where had that come from? She was not
boring. She was simply a reasonable person in control of her own life. What was wrong with that? Just
because her days—and nights—were a little more
bogged down in work and routine than she'd like them
to be, that didn't mean there was anything wrong. She
liked her life, there was no reason to change it, she—

Her fingers slipped. She hit a series of meaningless
keys that sent a row of nonsense running across the
screen. Exasperated, she cleared the line and scrolled
back the document to make sure she hadn't lost anything. It looked fine and she was just about to move
on to another when a name caught her eye.

Consolidated Trust, Ltd. What was that, a sup-
plier, an investor, a customer? She couldn't remem-

ber, but she knew she'd come across it before and it had stuck in her mind for some reason. Now it jumped out at her again, making her pause.

The name meant nothing. There was absolutely no reason to believe anything was wrong. She should go on, do the job by the book and get it done.

Except, a niggling little feeling was growing in her, an instinct, a tiny voice whispering that she should look closer.

She'd heard that voice before over the years. Sometimes it led nowhere, but not always. Sometimes it was right on target.

Consolidated Industries. She typed it in and hit the universal search command on the menu. Thank heaven for computers. Thank heaven for the scanners that had input the reams of documentation into neat little files she could comb through with a few key strokes. Thank heaven for—

Sheer luck. There it was again, on a record of payment for various miscellaneous services. The payment was for just under ten thousand dollars, low enough that the transaction didn't have to be reported at the time it occurred. It could be tossed in with all the jumble of other similar transactions, including dozens more to Consolidated Industries.

Kincaid must do a lot of business with them. But they were consistently paid in five-digit amounts, always just under the reporting threshold. Even so, the total added up to several million dollars paid out over just the past twelve months.

There could be any number of explanations, almost all of them perfectly legitimate. Still, it bore watching. She would have to see if there was a similar pattern anywhere else.

She was doing that, wandering through the maze of information that slowly but surely would become clearer to her, when there was a knock at the kitchen door.

Startled, Nora glanced at the clock. It was just after noon. Absorbed as she was, she'd lost track of time. Jumping up, she went to answer the door.

"Hi." Fletcher was wearing khakis, a blue denim shirt and a smile. He filled the doorway, all broad shoulders and long limbs. A basket swung from his hand. "Ready to go?"

"Oh, yes, sure. I just need to turn off the computer. Come on in."

He stepped into the kitchen, bringing with him the scent of the day, all sea air and sunshine. "How's your work going?"

"Pretty well, actually. I'm surprised by how much I got done."

"How come?"

Nora shut down the system, something she always did even if she was leaving only temporarily. Doing it here, in such an isolated setting, made her feel a little silly, but habits die hard.

She hesitated. She was surprised because she'd had such a hard time at first thinking of anything other than him. But this didn't seem like the time to say so. "I'm just not used to so much quiet."

He looked at her thoughtfully. "Maybe it'll grow on you."

"I don't expect to be here that long. Shall we go?"

He held the door for her. Nora locked it behind them. As she pocketed the key, she said, "I suppose people this far off the beaten track don't bother much with security."

"They still lock their doors. After all, this isn't exactly the far side of the moon."

"I guess not. But it is different." That was putting it mildly. The sunlight filtering through the trees fell like the pillars of an otherworld cathedral toward ground carpeted with soft green moss. The air was perfumed by the sea, mingling with the scent of the pine trees and all the other myriad fragrances of spring. The effect was heady. She breathed in deeply and closed her eyes for a moment.

When she opened them again, Fletcher was watching her. "You like it."

"Is that a question?"

"No."

He laughed at her surprise and reached out a hand. Nora hesitated only an instant before taking it.

They walked down a path softened by layers of fallen pine needles. Ahead, golden in the sunlight, was the beach. Gentle waves washed over the white sand and against the rock outcropping.

The tide was going out. Gulls circled overhead, calling raucously as they fed on the beds of mussels, their black shells glistening like polished stones.

Sandpipers raced back and forth at the waves' edge, their wand-slim beaks pecking.

"We're less than thirty-five miles from New York City," Fletcher said quietly. "Five miles from the center of one of the busiest suburban towns on the East Coast. But you'd never know it, would you?"

Nora shook her head. If she really strained to hear, she could just make out the faint sound of a boat far off on the Sound. Apart from that, there was only the gentle whisper of waves and wind, and the call of the birds.

"It must have looked a lot like this when the first white settlers came," she said.

"Almost identical. We have drawings, charts, written descriptions of Daniels' Neck, all indicating that it's virtually unchanged from the mid-seventeenth century, except for minor modifications to the house and the bridge that had to be built after the hurricane."

They continued walking in the direction of a copse of trees that extended on a small point out into the water. Fletcher's hand was warm and strong. By comparison, her own felt uncharacteristically small and delicate, the bones fragile and the skin much softer. Yet the impression was illusory. She was none of those things. She knew that and she suspected he did, too.

There was still something undeniably sweet and exciting about being with him, alone in this place that seemed set apart from the real world.

It was cooler in the copse. Shadows lingered among the sentinel pines. If possible, it was even quieter. Fletcher set the picnic basket down. He removed a plaid blanket and spread it over the ground.

With a flourish, he said, "Milady, your table awaits."

They sat cross-legged, looking out toward the Sound. Fletcher unpacked. There was a bottle of mineral water with a hint of lemon, a platter of sandwiches on freshly baked bread, vine-ripened cherry tomatoes and soft chocolate chip cookies that tasted as though they had just come from the oven, all magically emerging from the picnic basket.

Nora looked at him in disbelief. "I was expecting beef jerky and granola bars."

"Really? Here, try some of the ham with honey mustard. It's smoked over apple wood."

"Well, gosh, I'd hope so. What's this on top?"

"A garnish of paper-thin radish slices. They balance the sweetness, give it a little snap."

"Snap?"

"Crackle, pop."

He was laughing at her; she could see that in his eyes. Trouble was she didn't mind. "Do you always cook like this?"

"This? Don't tell me you're impressed?"

"Morbidly. If you also iron, I may be in serious trouble."

Had he been that close before? His eyes were the most incredible shade of blue surrounded by thick, sun-tipped lashes. And his mouth...

"Nora?"

"Yes?" Was that her voice? It seemed to be coming from so far away.

"You're a very lovely woman."

"Thank y—"

His mouth looked so hard yet felt so soft. The contradiction enthralled her. He was slow, presuming nothing, undemanding. Gently, even tenderly, he coaxed her response.

Either he was the most intuitively sensitive man she'd ever encountered or he'd had a tremendous amount of practice. She couldn't tell which. Perhaps the truth lay somewhere in between. Wherever, whatever, she loved the taste and touch of him. He drew her out of herself, bringing her to him so naturally that the kiss seemed as much her idea as his.

Instinctively she relaxed against him, her lips parting. She heard a groan but was unsure which of them the sound came from. Not that it mattered. She was lost in the moment and the man.

Her hands stroked the broad length of his back, feeling the play of muscle and sinew beneath the cotton shirt. The need to be closer to him—and closer still—rose in her. She arched against him, whispering his name.

He murmured something incoherent and moved so that she was under him, the blanket against her back and the sky above. His hands were slipping beneath her sweater to lightly cup her breasts. Their legs moved together urgently, hers parting, his thrusting between. His tongue drove deep, meeting hers, tasting and savoring.

Hunger roared through her, up out of a deep cavern of need she had never before realized existed. It eclipsed everything else—sanity, caution, the habits of a lifetime.

Metal rasped against her skin. She reached down, her fingers curling around the buckle of his belt. Urgently, without thought, she began to undo it.

A sudden wind blew through the pine trees, scattering needles, bending branches. Rain followed, without warning, cold and hard.

Chapter 8

"Come on," Fletcher said. They jumped up, tossed everything back into the picnic basket and ran for it. The rain came in sheets so heavy they could barely see. In moments, they were drenched.

Nora shivered, but not entirely from the cold. She was stunned at how close she had come to making love with him, this man she had known only a few days and who she still actually knew very little about. How could she possibly have been so impulsive, so foolish, so careless?

The thought that she was actually capable of such behavior—indeed, could welcome it without hesitation—stunned her. Even as they ran across the beach and toward the path leading back to the house, she felt as though the ground was rocking beneath her.

Nothing seemed certain anymore. The rules and standards she had always lived by were inadequate suddenly. She couldn't be sure of anything—except that she desperately needed to get a grip on herself before the situation slipped completely beyond her control.

At the end of the footpath, before they reached the house, Nora stopped. Fletcher's Jeep was parked a few yards away. Rain trickled down his cheeks and made his hair cling to his head in gleaming tendrils. His eyes were darker than usual, cautious and thoughtful.

Softly she said, "All things considered, I think we should skip the picnic."

"Is that what you want?"

No, it wasn't. What she wanted was to lie in bed with him and listen to the rain lash against the windows until the aftermath of passion carried her into sleep. But what she wanted now and what she would be able to live with come morning were two entirely different things.

"I think it's for the best."

He stared at her a moment longer, not angry or objecting, but still with that same thoughtful look. Finally he nodded. "You're probably right."

The ease with which he accepted her decision caused a tiny pang deep down inside her, but Nora ignored it. "Thanks for the tour."

He opened the Jeep's door and set the basket on the passenger seat. Over his shoulder, he said, "There's a lot more you might want to see."

"If there's time before I leave."

He nodded and got behind the wheel. Once more, he hesitated. Quietly he said, "If you need anything, I'll be around."

The promise warmed her. She had to fight the sudden urge to forget her best resolve and ask him to stay. "Of course you will be. You've got to look after the owls."

"The owls . . . right." He turned the key, looked at her once more and drove off.

Nora watched him go. It wasn't until the Jeep disappeared over the bridge and down the road that the rain finally drove her inside.

She left her sodden clothes on the bathroom floor, towel-dried her hair and wrapped herself in her favorite old robe. Back downstairs, she put the teakettle to boil, then went through the house turning on all the lights. The rain had lessened a little, but the storm seemed to have settled in for the long haul.

Fighting a surge of melancholy, she finished making the tea and sipped it as she stared at the computer screen. She had to get back to work. There were deadlines, reports, expectations. Kincaid Industries was turning out to be more complicated than she'd thought. She couldn't afford to waste time.

Besides, work was exactly what she needed, good, hard, interesting, all-consuming work. It had been her most reliable refuge all her life and there was no reason why it wouldn't be now. All she had to do was concentrate.

Not the easiest thing to accomplish when her imagination kept conjuring up crystalline blue eyes, taut muscles and that oh-so-tempting smile. Not easy at all.

But she did it, if only partly. While a defiant chunk of her mind remained focused on Fletcher, most of the rest managed to keep itself on her task. She got through a fair batch of files before the rumbling from her stomach reminded her that she'd had almost nothing to eat all day.

Added to all the other regrets she'd been having were those ham sandwiches—the ones with honey mustard topped by thin slices of radishes. Rummaging around in the freezer for something she could warm up, she sighed. She'd been rude to Fletcher, not even inviting him in out of the rain. But they both knew where that would have led and she simply wasn't ready. The odds were she never would be.

He was just . . . what? Too compelling, too disturbing, too passionate, too all the things she'd ever secretly wanted in a man but hadn't even hoped of finding. Too shattering to her peace of mind and what passed for security in a turbulent world.

Could she stand macaroni again? Gramma Liz had never put in a microwave. The regular oven would take ages. Thank heaven she'd had the foresight to buy a few cans of tuna fish.

Half an hour later, eating tuna out of the can, she stared blankly at the computer screen. It had gone to the screen saver that merrily depicted flying toasters. She could see her own reflection against the black background.

She was still sitting there, trying to muster enough interest to make toast, when the phone rang.

Her pulse jumped. Fletcher? No, it couldn't be. After the way she'd let him go, why would he call? Maybe to remind her to check up on the owls? No, he could do that well enough himself. It had to be someone else.

It was. The voice on the other end bore no resemblance at all to Fletcher's deep but invariably gentle tone. This man spoke more loudly, with that buoyant good nature that is supposed to denote confidence.

"Miss Delaney? Bob Kincaid. I heard you were in the neighborhood and I thought I'd give you a call. I'm having a little party Saturday. You'd be welcome to attend."

Nora held the receiver out and stared at it. Bob Kincaid—actually J. Robert Kincaid, CEO of Kincaid Industries—was calling to invite *her* to a party? Extraordinary. Maybe the White House would be on the line next to suggest she drop by next time she was out that way.

"Party?"

"That's right. Just a couple of dozen friends and neighbors. We are neighbors now, you know. I'm just a mile or so down the beach from you."

"Is that so? Gee, I didn't even know you lived in Belle Haven."

"Moved in about a year ago. Great little place. Love it. So are we set for Saturday?"

"Wouldn't miss it. What time?"

"Sevenish. Bring a friend if you like."

"Thanks, maybe I'll do that." It didn't seem appropriate to ask if there was anything else she could bring—bottle of wine, casserole, a little dessert. J. Robert undoubtedly had his needs seen to quite adequately.

"Super, bye."

Super. The man said super. Well, wasn't that nice? A party right down the beach, lots of new neighbors to get to know and probably great food. As for the little matter that she was involved in the audit of J. Robert's company, one thing had nothing to do with the other.

Right.

The tuna fish had lost appeal. She dumped it into the garbage and rinsed out a few dishes absently while mulling over the call. On the surface, there was nothing improper about it. They were neighbors, after all. She had to get used to the idea of that. With hindsight, she realized she had not considered all the ramifications of her inheritance, or perhaps she had simply decided to ignore them.

Whatever the case, the fact was that Amelia's house was not merely a family legacy or an interesting historic site. It was a lovely seafront home on a very large piece of land in one of the wealthiest and most expensive communities in the country. Naturally its new guardian would attract the interest of surrounding residents.

There was no reason to assume that Kincaid's invitation had anything at all to do with the audit. He might very well be unaware that she was even involved in it.

She could go with a clear conscience, have a good time and perhaps meet a few interesting people.

And she didn't have to go alone.

Not that she hadn't done that plenty of times in the past. Going places by herself was never a problem. She enjoyed her own company, but she also found it easy to talk to people she'd just met. That was the legacy of a childhood and adolescence spent moving around from one army posting to another. You either learned to relax and fit in with the group or you were sunk.

Going alone would be fine. But on the other hand... Her eyes drifted to the telephone, but she didn't pick it up. It was too soon and she still had too many doubts. Better to wait until she'd had a chance to think things over.

The rain was getting heavy again. Nora shivered and pulled the robe closer around herself. She thought of attempting another fire, but decided she wasn't up for the excitement.

Instead she went back to work. Maybe it was her imagination, but the files seemed a little more curious, a little more unusual now that she'd talked with Kincaid. She was starting to get the feeling that this assignment might not turn out to be quite so run-of-the-mill.

But, as yet, that was only instinct; she really had nothing to back it up, not even the payments to Consolidated, which might have a perfectly simple explanation.

Still, she stuck with it, getting up only to make more cups of tea. Evening came and with it early darkness because of all the clouds. Nora fiddled with the radio, found a classical music station and let it keep her company as she continued to search.

Hours passed. Every time she thought she was ready to quit, she came across something just interesting enough to keep her going. Nothing big, nothing startling, but more details in the picture she was building of how Kincaid Industries—and by extension, J. Robert Kincaid himself—worked.

He wasn't an orderly man. That much she could figure out already. Everything he touched generated enormous complexity. Was that merely his nature or did he do it deliberately to make his tracks more difficult to follow? She had no idea, but she was certain of one thing, before this was over she would know the answer.

But it would take more than a day—or a night. Rubbing the back of her neck, she glanced at the old wooden clock on the counter and was surprised to see that it was close to midnight.

She was very tired. Her eyes felt bleary and she had the beginnings of a headache.

Before it could get a hold on her, she switched the computer off and headed for bed. Kincaid and the files would still be there in the morning. So would the house and all it involved.

She was going to have to make decisions soon, decide how to deal with the family, with herself. But not just now.

Now was the wide, soft bed and the rain-swept night. Snuggling under the covers, she reached for the book she'd left on the table. *The Women of Belle Haven.* With a smile, she settled down to read herself to sleep.

Chapter 9

Arms closed around her, drawing her against firm, bare skin. Warm hands stroked her back, down the slender line of her spine to her buttocks. Muscled thighs moved over hers. A knee thrust between her legs, parting them.

Nora cried out. Her breasts ached, the nipples hot and firm. Liquid heat pooled at the center of her being. She couldn't lie still, had to move, had to find relief for the hunger savaging her.

His hair felt clean and thick beneath her fingers. The heat rolling off him engulfed her. She could smell crisp soap, a hint of citrus, all man. She opened her eyes, desperate to see him, but there was only darkness and distantly, tiny pinpoints of light.

Coolness flooded over her. Nora gasped and jerked upright. Her heart hammered against her ribs. She could hear her own ragged breathing.

She was alone in the bed in Amelia's house, in the night. Somehow she'd kicked the covers off. The rain had stopped and the sky was clear, revealing a sea of stars. But the cool air coming in through the window she'd left slightly open made her shiver all over.

That and the memory of a dream more passionate and enthralling than any she had ever experienced.

She managed to get out of bed to shut the window and find her robe, but by the time she'd done that, she was trembling. Her legs felt too weak to hold her. She sat down again on the edge of the bed, her arms wrapped around herself, and tried to calm down.

It wasn't easy. The dream had shocked her, not merely for its explicitness, but for the lingering grip it still seemed to exert. She could almost feel him moving against her, all tensile strength and hard, straining muscles, feel her own eager surrender.

A gasp broke from her. She pressed her fingers to her lips. What was happening to her? She had all the usual urges, but never would she have believed herself capable of such complete and unrestrained passion. That it had happened in a dream should have been some relief. Instead it only bewildered her all the more.

She turned slightly and glanced at the bed. It looked so soft and inviting. She could slip back down into it so easily, but the dream would be there waiting for her, she was sure of it. The temptation pulled at her, growing with each passing moment, almost irresistible.

With a start, Nora jumped up. She walked away from the bed, uncertain what to do or why she had to do anything at all. From a safer distance, she stared again at the high four-poster heaped with lace-edged pillows and a matching coverlet, the sheets scented with last summer's lilac.

On the floor beside the bed, unnoticed until now, was the book she had been reading. She picked it up and stared at the cover. The women of Belle Haven. She hadn't gotten very far into the story before sleep overcame her, but she had read enough to realize that the book wasn't at all what she'd expected.

A faint smile eased the tension from her mouth. No wonder Patrick Delaney's story sold so well. He had spun a tale of illicit love, great daring, shocked society and tumultuous but happy endings. They were the elements usually found in fiction, but if he was to be believed, everything he'd written was true. Moreover, it had happened to her ancestresses.

Nora shook her head wryly. Here she'd been thinking of them as strong, sensible women given to tending their herb gardens and their families. And so they had, but there was definitely another side to the women of Amelia's house, starting with Amelia herself. A definite tendency to love passionately if not always conventionally, to pledge heart and soul to men of enormous strength and will, and to dare all to make love endure.

Was it any wonder that she had dreamed of desire when so many of the women who had passed under this same roof had been driven by it?

That was it, obviously. It was the book that had prompted her dream, not thoughts of Fletcher.

Well, okay, maybe he'd been mixed up in it somewhere, but she wasn't going to dwell on that. Neither was she going back to bed. There was no point.

Instead she went downstairs. The house was quiet except for a few creaks and murmurs that she was getting used to. Shadows looming in the unlit hallway held no danger for her. She moved through them easily, not thinking until she reached the kitchen how very much at home she already felt in Amelia's house. If there were ghosts there—and considering how much life had reverberated within these old walls there might well be—they were gentle and benign. She felt no fear of them, only a sense that they added to the rightness of it all, to the feeling that this was where she belonged.

Except that she didn't. The little computer sitting on the kitchen table was enough to remind her of that. She had her life in the wider world, beyond the shelter of the centuries-old house and the secluded land around it. Beyond dreams that she wasn't completely sure were even her own.

Resigned that she'd had as much sleep that night as she was going to get, Nora put the kettle on. As it began to simmer, she turned on the computer and booted up the files she'd been studying earlier. If she couldn't rest, she might as well try to get a little ahead on work.

When the water was hot, she chose a herbal tea from Gramma Liz's collection and made herself a cup. It tasted of raspberries and summer. Sipping it, she continued trying to find her way through the maze of Kincaid Industries, wondering all the while if she was searching for something that didn't exist.

Outside, the night deepened. Wings fluttered in the branches of the old oak tree. The owl had hunted well.

In the blind below, the camera whirled softly, then went still. Fletcher ejected the film cartridge and inserted another, all with a minimum of sound. He'd remembered belatedly that the film would need to be changed. If he'd thought about it earlier, he could have done it then. But somehow it had slipped his mind.

Which explained what he was doing there at that hour of the night, checking up on the owls and trying not to think about the woman he supposed was asleep only a short distance away.

He'd behaved impulsively in the copse of trees by the beach. He didn't usually do that. Women liked him, they always had, but he couldn't ever remember trying to take advantage of that. He liked them, too, too much to behave carelessly. Until today. No, yesterday. Midnight had come and gone, bringing a new day.

Crawling out of the blind, he glanced toward the east. It would be dawn in a few hours. He was tired but not unduly so. There was an energy in him, a sense of mingled excitement and hunger, that kept weariness at a distance.

She had smelled of honeysuckle and, faintly, of mint. Her skin was warm, creamy soft, infinitely responsive. He remembered how she had moved against him, the fire he had felt in her, and groaned.

This had to stop. He was a sane, sensible man of the late twentieth century. He had a life that suited him well, work he cared about, his share of good friends, much to be grateful for. If there were times when he felt a strange sense of emptiness, a yearning he couldn't quite name, well, who didn't?

Someday, if he was lucky, he would meet the right woman. She would probably be in a line of work similar to his own. They'd have a great deal in common. It would be natural to stitch their lives together and build a future together. There wouldn't be all this turmoil and passion, this confusion and hunger.

The owl called above. Fletcher looked up, smiled wryly. There was blood on the bird's talons, gleaming darkly in the starlight. With a flutter of wings, it vanished into the darkness to hunt again.

That was nature—violent, sudden, primal. Humans were different. They had to be or they were damn well going to end up destroying the planet. Emotion had to be controlled, even denied. Reason counted for everything.

He'd forgotten that momentarily with the sound of the sea in his ears and Nora in his arms. But now, with the cool night air moving over him, he could remember it clearly enough. He would go back to the cabin and get some more sleep. In the morning, he had reports to see to, a paper to finish writing.

She'd made her feelings clear. He should be glad that of the two of them, she'd retained some sense. They knew so little about each other. It was madness to come together like that, in the heat and the passion, without thought.

Madness.

He shook his head, trying to clear it. Far out, beyond the trees, water gleamed darkly. No sound intruded, no hint of the modern world. It might have been centuries ago in a time long vanished yet still there, just beyond touch.

Weariness washed over him. He was very tired suddenly. With a sigh, he turned away, meaning to head for the Jeep and make his way home. But before he could do so, he noticed the light shining in the kitchen windows.

It hadn't been on when he'd come, he was sure of that. But it was there now, golden against the darkness. As he watched, he thought he saw a faint movement beyond, a slender shape to which his body responded instinctively.

Why would she be awake at this hour? Was there some further problem with the house? Was she sick? Or merely unhappy in the ill-defined way of emptiness and wondering?

He had to go. The Jeep was there, the cabin not many miles off.

She had made her feelings clear.

Turn away, go. He had no claim on her, no right to intrude.

But the light held him, beckoning against the darkness. Hardly realizing what he was doing, he walked toward it.

Chapter 10

Nora raised her head. Something had changed, she could feel it. The night, the silence, all remained. Yet nothing was the same.

Slowly she pushed her chair back and stood up. The computer screen glowed bright, neat rows of numbers parading across it, but she was unaware of it suddenly. Her eyes shifted to the kitchen door.

Beyond, so softly that she thought she was imagining it, she heard a step. And another. Closer.

Without thought, she walked over to the door. Her hand closed on the cool, smooth knob. She turned it.

Her first thought—if it could be called that—was gladness. It flowed through her, hot and fierce. She could feel herself smiling and couldn't stop.

"You're up late." Oh, brilliant! Couldn't she have thought of something better to say other than the obvious?

"You, too." At least he wasn't any more articulate.

"Is anything wrong?" Fletcher asked.

She could feel herself flushing, looked away quickly for just a moment. "No, I'm fine. Sometimes I like to work at night."

It wasn't exactly a lie. There were times when she'd done her best work in the late hours. But it wasn't her usual preference and she certainly hadn't planned on doing it here.

"Sorry to have bothered you then. I thought..." He turned as though to go.

"It's no bother," she said quickly. "What brings you out at this hour?"

He smiled a little self-consciously. "I forgot to change the film."

Forgot. His beloved owls, those fascinating creatures for whom he'd spent three days living in the blind waiting for their babies to hatch. Forgot.

Nora smiled. She stood aside, opening the door further. "I just made some tea. Would you like some?"

In the end, she made coffee. They sat and talked.

"I'm sorry," Nora said. "I behaved badly and I regret it. It's just that I wasn't prepared to deal with anything like that."

"There's no need to apologize. I was out of line. You're a terrific woman—intelligent, interesting, beautiful. But you're right. Neither of us wants to do something we'll regret later."

Nora put a spoon of sugar into her coffee, realized too late that she'd already done that and sighed. She got up to rinse out the cup. Standing at the sink, she said, "I'm not beautiful."

His eyebrows went up. "Oh?"

"I've got a good mind and I suppose I can be interesting when I try. But I'm definitely not beautiful."

He looked at her for what seemed like a long time but really couldn't have been more than a few moments. Gently he said, "Maybe we'd better talk about something else."

Nora agreed. She felt almost absurdly happy but safer, too, as though the ground was suddenly firmer under her. Sitting down again, she said, "I got a call from Bob Kincaid. Do you know him?"

Fletcher thought for a moment. "Fiftyish, silver hair, looks like a banker, lives down the beach a couple of miles?"

"That's him. He's giving a party Saturday." She took a deep breath. "I was wondering if you'd like to go."

He sat back, eyes crinkling at the corners, long legs stretched out in front of him, and regarded her. "You're asking me out?"

"It sounds like I am. But it's just a party, no strings. I'll have you home by midnight."

"Promise?"

"Cross my heart."

"Well, all right then."

They laughed, both of them, at the same time. Silence fell, but without strain. Finally Fletcher asked, "What's worrying you about Kincaid?"

"Worrying? What makes you think I'm worried?"

He shrugged. "I don't know. You just seemed that way when you mentioned him."

"And you didn't just put it down to my being nervous about asking you out?"

"Uh, no, actually I didn't. Should I have?"

"Maybe not." She hesitated. Her work had always been the kind that discouraged conversation. Aside from issues of confidentiality, most people just didn't want to know. How much could she—should she—say?

"Are you always this sensitive?" she asked, hedging.

"No."

Oh. Okay, she could deal with that and with the look in those crystalline blue eyes. That was all just fine.

"More coffee?"

"Sure, why not? I doubt I could get any more sleep tonight anyway."

Don't ask why. Don't say or do anything that would take the conversation back in the direction of what had almost happened out there by the beach scant hours before.

She poured, set the cups down on the table again and resumed her seat. Slowly she said, "I'm in the process of auditing Kincaid Industries."

"Does he know that?"

"I'm not sure. He knows my firm is handling it, obviously, but he wouldn't necessarily know which of us had been assigned."

"But he could?"

"Yes, he could."

"Maybe he's just being neighborly."

"That's how he made it sound," Nora acknowledged.

"But you're uncomfortable."

"Let's say I've got doubts."

"If he did know you're involved in the audit, would it be improper to socialize with him?"

"Not necessarily," she said. "Partners at the firm do it all the time."

"But you're not one of those."

"No . . . not yet."

He looked at her over the rim of the cup. "You'd like to be."

"I . . . don't know."

"Partner in a Big Six accounting firm? Isn't that like getting the brass ring?"

"Brass turns my skin green."

He laughed, a deep, male sound that sent a delicious little shiver up her spine. "So Mr. Kincaid may or may not know that you're working on the audit of his firm. If he does know, he may or may not care. Have I got it?"

"Perfectly. Do I sound paranoid?"

"No more than most city folks. Sounds like a fun party."

"There's just one thing..." He waited, a faint smile playing around that impossibly tempting mouth. "Being where it is and who's giving it, I'm guessing it's formal."

"Jeans won't cut it?"

"They do as far as I'm concerned. I just thought I should mention it."

She didn't want him to be embarrassed, but that wasn't likely to happen anyway. He was far too confident and self-possessed to worry much about the social niceties.

"I'll see what I can do," he said.

Nora glanced out the window, needing somewhere to look that wasn't at him. "It'll be light soon."

Softly he said, "This is my favorite time, right before everything starts, when anything is possible."

She turned back to him, watching the play of light and shadow across his features. There was a timelessness about him, she realized, giving a name to the vague impression that had been growing in her almost since their first meeting. He seemed less firmly rooted in the moment than other men she knew, less dependent on the modern world to give his spirit shape and meaning.

Sitting there, in the kitchen that was the heart of the old house, she had little difficulty imagining him in a different era. Perhaps it was the book she'd been reading, but she had the feeling he would be at home in those other times when the struggle for survival was so much more immediate, and men and women understood that they had to keep faith with each other or perish.

She shook her head, trying to throw off so odd a thought. History wasn't her favorite subject; she'd plowed through it in school and pretty much avoided it ever since.

She liked mysteries well enough, both those connected with her work and the paperback variety. But history had always seemed too dry a recital of dates and places, too lacking in color and texture.

Not the history of Belle Haven, though, or at least not the women of her family. That was anything but dry. There seemed a definite tendency to prefer men of a certain character, strong, demanding, passionate. She smiled faintly, wondering if it might be genetic.

"Want to let me in on the joke?" Fletcher asked.

With a start, she realized that he'd been watching her as she watched him. Warmth spread over her cheeks.

"No joke really. I was just thinking about a book I'm reading. It has to do with Belle Haven."

"Pat's book."

She stared at him in disbelief. "There's no way you could know that."

He sat back and regarded her with amusement. "Sure I could. First, there haven't been all that many books written about Belle Haven. Pat's is far and away the most popular. All the local bookstores have it and since it's almost entirely about women in your own family, it just stands to reason that's the one you'd pick up."

"Okay, you got me. Do you know Patrick Delaney?"

Fletcher nodded. "We go fishing together every once in a while. He's a nice guy."

"Not to mention a good writer."

"Yeah, that, too. But then he'd tell you himself that this was the one story he absolutely had to write—even if publishing it did drive the family crazy."

"Why?"

"They couldn't believe old Pat actually exposed the horrible truth. Not Liz, she didn't mind. But the rest of them went nuts."

Nora frowned. Granted, she'd only gotten through the first chapter or so, but she hadn't come across anything that merited describing in those words.

"What horrible truth?"

"That the women in your family—from Amelia Daniels on out—were real, flesh-and-blood people, not the plaster icons most of their descendants would like them to be."

"You can't mean the family was embarrassed? In this day and age?"

"You'd be surprised. Charlotte's not the only one who puts a whole lot of store in reputation. The Delaneys—and all the other branches of the family that are still around—are supposed to be models of rectitude, examples to everyone else, the inevitable leaders of the community, like that. They're not supposed to be giving birth to nine-pound babies six months after the wedding, like Amelia herself did, or getting caught up in a spy scandal like what happened to another, or for that matter running off with a half-Indian robber baron and then refusing to marry him when he tried to do the decent thing. That happened, too."

Nora took a deep breath. "Sounds like I'd better read the rest of that book fast."

"Personally, I took it slow. I didn't want to miss anything."

Great, he knew more about the women she came from than she did herself. And what he knew seemed to please him mightily.

She added another spoonful of sugar to her coffee and stirred it with exaggerated care, focusing all her attention on the swirling liquid and the clink of the spoon against the china.

"Under the circumstances," she said, "this makes Gramma Liz's decision to leave me the house all the more puzzling."

"How so?"

"You'd think she would have given it to someone more in keeping with family traditions, as it were."

"More like the women in the book."

She looked up, her eyes meeting his. "Exactly."

Try though she did, she couldn't decide whether his mouth was more attractive when he was smiling or when he appeared very serious as he did just now. It was a real toss-up.

"Are you sure she didn't?" he asked.

For once in her hardworking, detail-oriented, fact-dedicated life, Nora had no answer.

Chapter 11

The lawyer called shortly after nine. Fletcher had left several hours before and Nora had actually managed to go back to work. She was deep into yet another file on Kincaid Industries when the phone rang.

"Sorry to bother you," Jerome Sanders said, not in the usually perfunctory way but with a note of real apology that immediately made Nora alert. "I think we need to talk."

She pushed back from the table. It was a bright day outside. The sky through the kitchen window looked as blue as Fletcher's eyes.

Wrong, don't think of that. Focus on the moment, on what really matters. On business.

"Let me guess, you've heard from Charlotte."

Jerome made a faint sound—a little surprised, mostly relieved that he wouldn't have to explain quite everything. He was a young man, in his late twenties, a graduate of the same Yale Law School most of the men—and lately a few of the women—in his family had been going to for generations.

Nora vaguely knew that the Sanders' legal firm had been involved with the Delaney's—and various other branches of the family—for generations. She supposed there was little Jerome didn't know, or couldn't find out if he took the trouble. Much as she would have preferred a bit more privacy, it did make things easier.

"She called yesterday," he said, "and came by this morning."

"Already."

"With my morning coffee."

Nora laughed softly. "Oh, dear. All right, let's talk."

"First, you'd better understand it isn't just her. She can control a good deal of the family."

"I'll bet. So the story is that I somehow coerced Gramma Liz into leaving me the property and the will should be contested?"

"Too bad you went for accounting instead of law. You'd be very good at summation."

"Thanks. Does she have any grounds?"

There was silence for a moment before Jerome said, "Mrs. Delaney did alter her will shortly before her death to make you her principal heir. My father and I both consulted with her at the time. Any time a will is changed so close to the actual time of death questions are bound to be raised. But in this case—"

He hesitated. Nora took a deep breath. She had the feeling that she was going to really need Jerome Sanders's help but she didn't want to depend on him unless he could really commit himself to her side. Given his family's long involvement with her own, could he really do that?

"Mrs. Delaney had been indicating for some time that she wasn't happy with the idea of Daniels' Neck being left to a charitable foundation run by the family. She seemed troubled by the idea that the house would no longer actually be lived in. When she came in to make the necessary changes, she seemed genuinely happy, as though something that had been troubling her deeply was finally being resolved."

Nora's throat was tight. She had trouble speaking. "Gramma seemed happy?"

"Yes, she did. She spoke of you with great pride and love, said she should have done what she was doing years before." Jerome paused for a moment. Gently he said, "Look, I've talked this over with my father and we both have the same recollection, but you must realize, the family can bring in its own experts, people who will say she could have been unduly influenced."

"Would that be enough to overturn the will?"

"Probably not, but it could turn out to be a protracted battle. Is that what you want?"

"I don't know," Nora admitted. "At the moment, I'm not sure of much of anything."

"It's early yet," Jerome said. "You've had the shock of your grandmother's death and your sudden inheritance. It's only natural that you'd need time to think about what's happened."

It sounded as though he was rehearsing something he'd planned to say to someone else—Charlotte Delaney, most likely. Nora didn't mind. He was offering her a gracious—if temporary—out. She grabbed it.

"Surely anyone would understand that?"

"No doubt." Jerome hesitated. "At least for a while." He wasn't going to leave her in any doubt. Whatever reprieve she had would run out before too long.

"A while," Nora repeated. She supposed that meant a few weeks, not more. It puzzled her that she wished she could have longer. Hanging up the phone, she sat back in the chair and stared sightlessly at the computer screen.

What was the matter with her? Jerome didn't have to spell out for her the way things were. The family certainly didn't want a lengthy—and very public— battle over Gramma Liz's will. All Nora had to do was indicate that she was willing to turn the property over to the family foundation that had expected to inherit it in the first place. No doubt there would be immediate talk of appropriate compensation and so on. The family could well afford it. She would walk away a wealthy woman, and Daniels' Neck would be protected.

What could be better than that?

She stood up slowly and carried her coffee cup over to the sink. Staring out the window, her eye was caught by the flutter of tree branches in the breeze. It was a beautiful scene, peaceful, bucolic, exactly the sort of place she'd always avoided.

The problem was, she realized, it was so quiet she could hear all her thoughts. Not just the ones she chose to pay attention to but all of them, including that contrary little voice way down deep inside her that kept saying the heck with the family, Gramma Liz knew what she was doing.

Yeah, right. Pick a city kid who didn't even have the sense to open the fireplace flue to inherit an historical treasure.

No, not that. Gramma Liz's legacy was a house, a real, vibrant, strong house that was meant to be a home, not a museum.

There was no doubt what Gramma Liz had hoped for—even plotted—to achieve. Another of Amelia's descendants, another in the unbroken line of family women, who had made this house a home for so many generations, filling it with love, passion and tenderness.

With life.

Surely there had been someone—anyone—else in the family who would have been a better choice? Out of the nine grandchildren Charlotte had cited, wasn't there at least one who would have jumped at the chance to live in Amelia's house?

Yes, there probably was, but for some reason, Gramma Liz hadn't chosen any of them. She'd chosen Nora. Either she'd been completely mistaken or she just might have known something Nora didn't.

She took a deep breath and as she did, noticed her own reflection in the window. The woman who gazed back at her looked like a solemn pixie, all short hair and big eyes, appropriately framed between trees and clouds as though not quite of this world.

That wasn't her. It couldn't be. The light was playing tricks, or it was her own weariness and confusion. She was firmly rooted in reality, given to neither whimsy nor wishfulness.

Gramma Liz had been wrong, plain and simple.

Fine, then pick up the phone and call Jerome back. Arrange a meeting with Charlotte. It could all be said and done before the day was over.

And she could leave.

Walk away, not look back. Count her money and be glad.

Forget the whisper of wind in the ancient oak trees, the rhythm of the surf against the beach. The glint of blue eyes that seemed to see straight into her soul.

Forget walking away, she could run.

Except that she'd never done that in her life, never once ducked a battle, never given up. Not in all the new towns and new schools she'd known, not with all the new kids and new ways she'd constantly had to get used to. She'd held her head up, smiled and kept going. Always.

Sure, there had been times when she thought she just couldn't do it anymore. On the shelf of the bedroom closet in her apartment—where she could still see it every time she opened the door—was the battered old bear that had absorbed more tears than anyone could count. She'd been lonely, confused and sad. But she'd also known real happiness and pleasure in meeting the challenges she'd been thrown and for the most part handling them well.

They'd made her the person she was today. If she had any regrets, it was that she'd never really told her father what a good job he'd done helping her through them. She'd been eight when her mother died in a car crash. Peter Delaney had been left to pick up the pieces and get on with life as best he could. All things considered, she thought he'd done a good job. It occurred to her that she'd never really told her father that.

On impulse, she reached for the phone again. With a quick glance at the clock to mentally compute the time in Saudi Arabia, she punched in a series of numbers.

Lieutenant Colonel Peter Delaney, retired, answered on the second ring. At the familiar sound of his voice, Nora felt herself relaxing.

"Hi, Dad, how're you doing?"

"Hey, peanut!" He was the only person who called her that, absolutely the only one. "What's up?"

"I just thought I'd give you a call. Does there have to be a special reason?"

"You know there doesn't. I'm always delighted to hear from you. But since this isn't the second or fourth Monday of the month—"

Nora laughed. For years, ever since she'd left for college, they'd had the same schedule. Twice a month, as regular as clockwork, they checked in with each other.

Unless something unusual happened. She'd called him when Gramma Liz died and of course, they'd been together at the funeral. He knew the contents of the will, but there hadn't been a chance for them to talk about it. Now she could hear the curiosity in his voice, and the concern.

"What's up, kid?"

"The family's gearing up to contest the will."

He made a sound of disgust. "That would be Charlotte, of course."

"I gather she's not alone."

"Let them contest all they want. I'd bet money that Mom had the legalities tied up tighter than a brass drum."

"It probably doesn't matter. Keeping this house would be a crazy idea."

"You think so?"

"I'm not exactly a country girl."

"Oh, I don't know. Maybe you just never had the chance."

"No, Dad, take my word for it. My first night here, I almost set fire to the place."

"What?"

"I forgot to open the fireplace flue."

"Nora, you know better—"

"No, I didn't, that's the point. If it hadn't been for Fletcher, who knows what would have happened."

"Fletcher?"

Uh-oh, tactical error. She hadn't meant to mention Fletcher. Or had she?

"He's a naturalist. Gramma Liz was letting him study some owls that are nesting near the house."

"Naturalist...owls?"

Her father sounded genuinely bewildered, as though what he was hearing made absolutely no sense. But then it wasn't exactly logical to Nora, either.

"He's not one of those tree huggers, is he?"

"I think he probably cares a lot about the environment, if that's what you mean."

"Nice little guy, skinny, glasses, like that?"

Nora laughed. "No, not exactly."

"Hmm, tell me more."

"There's nothing to tell. He helped me, probably saved the house, that's all. The point is I don't know what I'm doing here. Well, I do, but I shouldn't stay. It's crazy, except I hate to let Gramma Liz down. She really wanted someone to live here and she picked me. The rest of the family wants to turn the place into a museum."

"Of course they do. Think of the tax write-off."

Nora's mouth opened, closed, then opened again. Holy cow, did she feel dumb.

"Dad, I didn't think of that."

Peter Delaney's incredulity reached her clear over the thousands of miles of telephone hookup. "Come on, honey, of course you did. You're an accountant."

"It should have occurred to me, but it honestly didn't. I've been so busy thinking about Gramma and the house, and—"

"The tree hugger? What's his name again?"

"Fletcher, Hamilton Fletcher. But I haven't been—"

"Sean Fletcher's nephew?"

"I don't know, he never said— That is, he grew up in New York City, but he mentioned he had family here."

"I'll say he did. The Fletchers go way back. Heck, I knew Sean pretty well. He was okay."

"What happened to him?"

"Drowned trying to rescue some damn fool tourists who took a boat out into a nor'easter. Muscular guy, blond-haired, liked to shoot pool. His nephew anything like him?"

"Uh . . . I don't know about the pool."

"Listen, peanut, I know you're a big girl now and all that but I'm still your father. Frankly those suits you've introduced me to every once in a while never came across as much. Tree hugger or not, if this guy's got his priorities straight, he might be okay."

"Okay for what, Dad?" Nora asked, even though she was sure of the answer.

"You know for what. I'm not going to be around forever."

"Dad—"

"No, listen to me. It's a tough world out there. You shouldn't have to deal with it alone. I've always hoped—" He stopped, as though catching himself.

Gently Nora said, "Go on, Dad."

She could hear him take a deep breath over all those miles. He was a man who didn't express deep feelings easily, at least not with words. It was a mark of how much he cared that he was willing to try now. "I want you to have a family, Nora. A real one with a husband you can count on and kids of your own. That's what makes life worth living."

"There are people who would disagree with you."

"Yeah, but they're wrong."

She laughed despite the sheen of tears in her eyes. He never changed, her father. He was always the same, straight talking, firm in his opinions, but still gentle and loving.

"I've got a feeling you might like Fletcher. He's pretty much okay, for a tree hugger, that is."

"He doesn't really... I mean, he wouldn't actually..."

"Maybe just a little peck on the bark every once in a while."

Her father sighed, the long-suffering sound of the bewildered male. "I don't suppose you'd like to meet a fine, upstanding cargo pilot I play poker with?"

"Let me guess, long haul runs Stateside to Saudi, drinks Lone Star beer, roots for the Cowboys, has those reflector sunglasses. Name's—hold on, it's coming to me—Chip, no, sorry, Chimp."

"I'm surprised at you, girl. I thought you were too good for that kind of stereotyping."

"You're telling me I'm wrong?"

She had followed a lifetime of her father's poker buddies. So far as she was concerned, they really were all the same.

"Name's Brad."

"What about the rest?"

"Vikings fan."

"You're kidding? Well, that makes a big difference."

"Okay, I'm never going to get to fix you up with someone. Probably just as well. But you make sure this Fletcher guy knows you've got a father in the wings."

"Dad, really—"

"And, honey, about the house, it's your decision, of course, but one thing I can tell you, Mom was a hell of a smart woman. She didn't make too many wrong calls."

Which did nothing at all for Nora's peace of mind. They talked a few minutes longer before hanging up. When she put the phone down, the silence was so complete that she could hear the grandfather clock ticking in the parlor.

Time was passing. She needed to do some hard thinking—about the house, about herself. And about Hamilton Fletcher.

She shook her head, still amazed that she'd invited him to go with her to Kincaid's. She'd never actually asked a man for a date before and when she finally did, it had to be someone so far removed from her own world. Kincaid and Fletcher. Tycoon and owl lover. Business and—

Okay, she needed to think, but not this minute. Work was there, right in front of her, always a ready refuge.

Besides, she had a valid reason to retreat into her computer files. Before she walked into Robert Kincaid's house, she intended to know as much about him as she possibly could.

Why exactly she felt the need to do that she couldn't have said, but if there was one thing she was learning, it was to trust her instincts.

All of them, including the ones she'd never known she had before.

Chapter 12

The grandfather clock was ticking again. Actually it ticked all the time, but Nora only noticed it occasionally. Like now.

Maybe it was true what they said about clocks. A watched one never boiled.

She giggled at the thought, caught herself doing it and pressed her fingers to her lips in surprise. She wasn't a giggler. A good hearty laugh now and again, sure, but never giggles. Or at least not since she'd grown out of training bras and acne cream.

And she was definitely out of both those now. Staring at herself in the hall mirror, she frowned. Maybe the dress wasn't a good idea. But it was one of the few she owned that could be considered at all formal, the only one she'd brought with her. Besides, it wasn't precisely revealing, just ... suggestive.

The high lace collar, fitted bodice, nipped-in waist and graceful midcalf-length skirt were all vaguely Victorian. The creamy ivory hue of the material brought out her coloring and made the foil of her short auburn hair all the more dramatic.

She'd avoided any obvious makeup but her amber brown eyes seemed to glow and she thought her mouth looked fuller than usual. Maybe that was because she kept chewing on the lower lip, a nervous habit she'd never been so troubled by as on this night.

She took a deep breath, struggling for calm. It was just a party. She'd been to dozens of similar events, mostly business occasions. They weren't her favorite thing to do, but she didn't hate them, either. There would be good food, decent music, interesting people. A few hours and she'd be home. No big deal.

Which, of course, neatly overlooked the whole issue of Fletcher. She glanced at the clock again. He wasn't even late yet and she was just about ready to jump out of her skin. This had to stop.

Determined, she went into the kitchen and began tidying shelves that really didn't need it, anything to keep her mind off the clock and the man. She'd just decided to do a little dusting in the pantry when two things happened simultaneously—the grandfather clock chimed eight and the doorbell rang.

Nora put down the duster, straightened her shoulders and went to answer it.

"Hi."

Hi? This... this cross between a Greek god and a Viking warrior appeared at her doorstep and said hi? No, that was wrong. Greek gods and Vikings didn't wear impeccably tailored evening clothes or come bearing bouquets of flowers.

"Hi." She was down to monosyllables, but at least she could get that much out instead of just standing there, gaping at him. In denim and plaid, he was gorgeous. But freshly shaved, hair curling slightly at his nape, with the dark evening clothes emphasizing the power of his body and the perfection of his chiseled features, he was downright devastating.

No fair, but then when had life ever been?

"Flowers," she murmured, focusing on them just a little frantically. Anything but look at him. "How nice."

She reached out and he put the flowers in her hands.

"I'll just put these in water," she murmured and beat a hasty retreat.

He followed. Casually, hands in his pockets, looking completely relaxed, he said, "That's a nice dress."

"What? Oh, this? Thanks, it's nothing." The flowers were drowning. She poured some of the water off and took a stab at arranging them in a vase. "These are beautiful, but you shouldn't have gone to the trouble."

She envisioned a trip into town, the search for a florist, decisions about what to pick. It was all very sweet and touching. Devastating.

"No trouble. They grow outside my cabin. I've been seeding around there with wildflowers for years. They've taken real well."

Oh, great, he'd picked them for her himself from flowers he'd practically planted—seeded, whatever. No fair. Men weren't supposed to look like that and still be so nice, to grow their own flowers and send tingles down her spine.

She set the vase on the kitchen table. A little water splashed out. Fletcher reached for a towel as Nora did the same. Their hands brushed.

She pulled back, but not before realizing that he had done the same and just as quickly. They stared at each other.

His eyes were hooded, but she could feel the heat in them. The skin across his cheekbones darkened slightly. With quiet steadiness, he said, "You look beautiful."

She met his gaze. "Thank you."

The water was mopped up, her shawl found, the porch light left on. Fletcher held the door for her. She locked it behind them. Together, they walked down the few steps to where he had left the Jeep.

As she got in, Nora said, "I still feel I should have picked you up."

He slid behind the wheel and turned the key. "Next time."

No fair. Her heart was speeding up again and she was back to feeling like a thirteen-year-old.

The night was star-draped. Not a cloud marred the sky as they traveled the few miles down the beach road to Robert Kincaid's house. High stone pillars and iron gates announced its presence. The gates stood open, but uniformed security guards were checking each car as it was admitted.

"Some house," Nora murmured as her name was checked off on the guest list.

That was an understatement. Robert Kincaid had himself a mansion of the variety rarely seen outside of television miniseries and glossy magazine spreads. Built of pale stone in the style of a French château, the house rose three graceful stories to a slate roof framed by brick chimneys. It was surrounded by rolling lawns and what looked to be elaborate formal gardens visible in the light spilling from every window.

"How old do you think it is?" Nora asked. The house was so large that she automatically associated it with another era, one with no sense of limits or, for that matter, proportion.

"Less than a year," Fletcher said, disabusing her of the notion. "Kincaid rolled into town flush from the stock market and eager to establish himself in a big way. He tried to buy Daniels' Neck."

Nora looked at him in surprise. "I had no idea of that."

"He wasn't the only high roller who wanted it. After all, it's the prime piece of real estate around here, sea views, undeveloped, the whole bit. But Liz sent him packing the same as she did all the rest. He had to settle for this spot."

"Not exactly a hardship. It's lovely."

"At least there was already a house here, one of those big, sprawling places put up in the 1920s. He tore that down and built what you're looking at."

"Did you bring the bread crumbs?"

"The what?"

"You know, leave a trail of bread crumbs. Otherwise how are we ever going to find our way out of there?"

Fletcher laughed. He look her arm, his touch warm, gentle, protective. And very arousing.

Nora closed her eyes for just an instant. She opened them to the light and noise spilling out of the double doors directly ahead of them. The party drew them in.

"Yum, yum," Fletcher said.

"Hmm," Nora agreed.

They were nibbling on chicken satay, little grilled bits of chicken in a peanutty Thai sauce. The perfect accompaniment to the fluted goblets of champagne being passed around by liveried waiters.

The room they were standing in ran most of the length of the house on the south side. Beyond it was a stone terrace that led down to lawns and gardens, and beyond them was the sea. High french windows led out onto the terrace. A fireplace large enough to walk into dominated one far wall while at the other a dais held a grand piano and other instruments, presently in use by a quartet of classical musicians.

Guests circulated, drinks in hand, waving and smiling when they spotted those they knew, keeping an eye

out for whoever else of interest might wander by even
while carrying on forcefully animated conversations.

Nora smiled and took a sip of the champagne. For
all the magnificent setting and elegant clothes, the
party reminded her of more than a few she'd been to
in the past, filled with people working hard to impress each other while trying to look as though they
were doing anything but.

There was a certain brittleness to it, even a hint of
desperation that would get her down if she let it. She
wouldn't. She was there to satisfy her curiosity and
have a good time. Besides, she was suddenly starving.

"You're a bad influence," she said when Fletcher,
correctly discerning her mood, pressed another of the
delicious little chicken things on her.

"I try my best," he agreed and smiled as she sighed
with pleasure. "Besides, we wouldn't want to insult
Mr. Kincaid by not eating his food."

"Speaking of, any idea where our host might be?"

Fletcher looked around. His greater height gave him
the advantage. He could see over practically everyone
else's head. "Over there," he said, gesturing in the
general direction of the massive fireplace.

"I suppose we should go say hello."

They put down their plates with some reluctance
and began making their way through the crowd. Other
people had clearly had the same idea. There was a
cluster of four, maybe five deep around Kincaid. He
appeared to be holding court.

"We'll never get near him," Nora said, eyeing the
big man. He was about the same height as Fletcher but

older by ten, perhaps fifteen years. He had the look of a weekend sailor, or more probably in his case, yachtsman, skin wind-burnished, crinkled around the eyes. His hair was silver, his evening dress perfect. He looking like Central Casting's idea of the wealthy, powerful businessman, except he was the real thing.

"You came to meet him, didn't you?" Fletcher asked.

"Yes, but..."

"Then come on."

She had no idea how he did it, but Fletcher moved a little this way, a little that, pressed a broad shoulder here, a hint of an elbow there and they were through. Before she knew it, Nora was standing directly in front of their host.

Kincaid smiled at her. "Hello." Contrary to the previous occasion when they'd spoken, his voice was now perfect, deep and smooth, congeniality and authority blended in equal proportions.

Fletcher took over. He introduced himself and Nora. For a moment, she was vividly aware of the currents passing between the two men, unable to fully understand them but conscious all the same of how they were assessing each other, two big, hard, confident men from very different worlds yet not without some elements in common.

Kincaid smiled first. He took Nora's hand and looked directly into her eyes. "I'm delighted you could come, Ms. Delaney. And you, too, of course, Mr. Fletcher."

If being passed off as an afterthought bothered Fletcher, he didn't show it. Nora was grateful for his quiet, watchful presence. She was surprised by her reaction to Robert Kincaid. He was more attractive than she had expected, more compelling.

And unless every instinct she possessed had suddenly evaporated, he seemed extremely interested in her.

Why? Because he knew she was involved with the audit of Kincaid Industries? Or because he still had some interest in acquiring Daniels' Neck?

"Fletcher," Kincaid was saying even as he continued to focus his attention on Nora. "You do something with animals, don't you?"

Studied them, nurtured them, protected them. Kincaid made it sound like he was cleaning up after the circus.

"You could say that," Fletcher replied. He seemed amused.

Kincaid smiled broadly. "There's someone here you've got to meet. Great guy, name's Charles Jefferson. I'm sure you've heard of him."

Fletcher nodded. "The philanthropist."

"That's right. Old Charlie's got it in his head that he wants to set up some kind of—what's he call it?— ark to protect endangered species."

Kincaid glanced around, saw who he was looking for and raised a hand. "Charlie, over here. Want you to meet Hamilton Fletcher, best damn animal protectionist in these parts. I'm sure the two of you have a lot to talk about."

The other man—shorter than Kincaid and carrying maybe twenty pounds he could have done without—looked surprised. He had a round, pleasant face and a hesitant smile, but his eyes held the gleam of intelligence—and dawning interest.

"Fletcher? You wrote the monograph on reintegration of peregrine falcons into the wild that was in *Biographics* last month."

Under other circumstances, Nora might have found Fletcher's response funny. He looked dumbfounded to encounter someone under these circumstances who actually knew his work, moreover who obviously cared.

"I did write that—"

"Damn fine piece. Bob's right, we should talk. I've been thinking that—"

Before Nora could fully grasp what was happening, Jefferson had gotten hold of Fletcher's arm and was steering him toward a quieter corner of the room, talking intently all the while.

Behind her, Kincaid laughed. "That's what I love to see, people making contact. Care for a glass of champagne, Ms. Delaney?"

Nora turned, looking at him steadily. Despite the other guests pressing around, trying to get his attention, he seemed to have no interest in anyone but her. Had things been different, she might have been flattered.

And truth be told, she was, if only a little. But she was also cautious. She was absolutely certain without

anyone having to tell her that Robert Kincaid wanted
something. The question was what?

"Champagne would be fine," she said and put on
her most professional smile.

Chapter 13

"Some view, isn't it?" Kincaid said. They were standing outside on the stone terrace. Behind them, the party continued in full swing. Nora was surprised at how easily her host had extricated them, but she gathered he had a lot of practice.

Robert Kincaid had been very successful for a lot of years. No doubt he had grown adept at sidestepping those who wanted his friendship, his power, or merely to be seen with him. He must have had to in order to get any time for himself—and his own wants.

"It's a beautiful house," she said. The champagne in her hand remained untasted. She wanted all her faculties clear.

"The architect did a nice job," he agreed. Leaning against the parapet that ran all the way around the terrace, he smiled at her. "Of course, you know I wanted to build it on Daniels' Neck."

His frankness startled her, but she did her best not to show it. "Really?"

"Sure, it's the best place around here. At the time, I'd just come up from the city and I didn't fully appreciate the, shall we say, sensitivity about that particular spot." He laughed. "Your grandmother set me straight quick enough. She sent me hightailing it back over that little bridge, glad to still have all my skin."

"I can't believe Liz was that rough on you," Nora demurred.

"Don't get me wrong, she was a real lady, your grandmother. But that piece of land was heaven on earth to her. She wasn't going to let anyone harm a twig of it."

"Do you blame her?"

"No, truth be told, I don't. Now that I know something about the history of the place, I can well understand her feelings."

"Besides, you certainly didn't do badly right here."

He nodded. They stood looking out toward the water. Nora waited, wondering how long Kincaid would be content to remain silent. Moments passed, no more.

"I hear the family's not too thrilled about you inheriting."

Nora set the champagne down on the parapet. She leaned back against the cool stone. A breeze off the Sound ruffled the lace edge of her skirt. "Where did you hear that?"

He shrugged. "It's around. Nasty business when families squabble over a will."

"If you don't mind, I'd prefer not to discuss it."

"Of course, excuse me. I shouldn't have brought it up. Whatever you do with the place is strictly your business." He paused briefly before he said, "By the way, am I right in thinking you work for—?" He mentioned the name of her firm.

"Yes, I do. As a matter of fact, I feel I ought to mention to you that I'm assigned to the audit on Kincaid Industries."

He looked amused. "You need to tell me that?"

"I'm more comfortable with you knowing." As she said that, Nora realized that she had no idea whether he'd known before or not. Nor was she clear on whether his interest in Daniels' Neck really had been put to rest.

"Okay, I know. If you have any questions, feel free to give me a call." He said it casually, an offer of assistance he would make as a matter of course.

"Thank you, but everything seems very complete." She saw no reason to mention her feeling that the records were too complicated, too many layers on top of too many others. The business had grown at an extraordinary pace. It might be expected to be less well organized than others.

Or less clearly organized. They weren't necessarily the same thing.

"Have you been doing this sort of thing for long?" Kincaid asked.

"Since I got out of school." Determined not to keep the focus on herself, Nora said, "How about you? Were you always a high-powered tycoon?"

He looked startled, then laughed. "Hell, yes, I was the most profit-oriented little four-year-old you ever saw. Did a leveraged buyout on a lemonade stand and never looked back."

Nora grinned. She couldn't help it. A sense of humor, particularly a self-deprecating one, was something she hadn't expected to find in a man like Robert Kincaid.

"Do you like having a lot of money?" she asked, suddenly serious. It was a question she had wondered about ever since she began studying money, where it came from, where it went. There were times when it seemed to take on an identity all its own.

"I like it better than not having any," he admitted. "But if you're asking does it make life perfect, far from it."

"I wouldn't be that naive. Still, there must be a great deal you get to do that makes life more interesting and satisfying."

He shot her a hard look, giving her a glimpse, she thought, of the real man behind the carefully crafted veneer. "You're very direct, Ms. Delaney. Most people—particularly women—never mention my money."

"I suppose that's because they want you to believe they're so captivated by your company they completely forget about how rich you are."

He gave a quick laugh and studied her with approval. "Are you always this frank?"

"Pretty much. I was an army brat. We tend to pick up good survival skills, but diplomacy isn't always one of them."

"But then, since you're doing the audit, you'd know how much money I've got, wouldn't you?"

Nora shrugged. She wasn't about to admit that when it came to the Kincaid Industries audit, she had a whole lot more questions than she had answers. Uppermost in her mind was the fact that she might be on the track of something that didn't exist. If she followed it too obviously, however, she risked offending an important client of the firm's and making a fool of herself in the process.

Better to hang back a little and assess the terrain before proceeding. Cautiously she said, "There's no doubt you've made a great success of your business."

His smile, she noticed, was just a shade too fast. It was more a baring of teeth than a display of good humor.

"What I've done so far," he said, "is nothing. The world's moving into a whole new era. There are going to be tremendous opportunities for those smart enough to spot them."

"And Kincaid Industries is poised to do so?"

"You've seen our books. Do you seriously doubt it?"

"No," Nora admitted. "But I'm just a bean counter. If the numbers add up right, I'm satisfied."

His smile deepened. He took a step closer, not so much that she could be tempted to pull back, but enough to make her even more aware of him.

"Really?" he asked. "That's all it takes."

A tiny spurt of surprise went off inside her. There was no doubt that Robert Kincaid was an attractive man, as well as an extremely rich and successful one. Unless she was very much mistaken, he had just made a mildly suggestive remark, nothing really offensive, but enough to create the impression that his interest in her was not purely professional—or neighborly.

She should have been at least a little pleased, flattered, whatever. Instead she merely felt impatient with herself for being in the situation in the first place.

Deliberately she looked past him to the house. "I'm afraid some of your other guests are feeling left out."

He shrugged, but shifted slightly so that he was no longer quite so close to her. "Half of them I don't even know and the other half—well, let's just say there's maybe a handful of people in there I actually like and enjoy being with."

"Then why invite all the others?"

"Because that's how business gets done. Your friend, for instance, what's his name—?"

"Fletcher."

"Him. He and Charlie are probably as happy as two hogs in mud to have each other to talk to. Who knows, maybe they'll put something together. In the meantime, what do you say we—"

"Go back inside? Good idea."

Nora jumped. Fletcher emerged from the shadows near the door without warning. His stride was long and lithe as he walked across the terrace.

"She's right," he said, looking at Kincaid. "Your guests are getting restless."

"How long have you been there?" Nora blurted. She felt foolish the moment the question was out, but she couldn't help it. The idea of him standing there, listening to them, watching, was deeply unsettling. Not the least because it made her feel something she hadn't in a very long time—protected.

Fletcher glanced at her. His eyes were unreadable. "Long enough. Nice party, Mr. Kincaid. You shouldn't miss it."

Nora breathed in sharply. This went beyond any sort of banter between men testing each other. Fletcher was challenging Kincaid directly and they both knew it. Incredibly it seemed to be over her.

"I really don't think—" she began.

"I'm glad you're enjoying yourself, Mr. Fletcher," Kincaid said smoothly. "But was it wise to leave Charlie in the lurch?"

"Actually I left him dancing with a real friendly blonde. Care to join them, Nora?" He held out his hand, a gesture that both beckoned and commanded.

She hesitated, unsure of what was happening or why, uncertain of how to handle it. This was the late twentieth century, for heaven's sake, men didn't do this sort of thing. Did they?

She would have to add that to the list of questions for which she seemed to have no answers. Or at least none she was ready to acknowledge. Yet for all that, some part of her mind seemed able to function inde-

pendently. Almost before she was aware of what she
was doing, Nora placed her hand in his.

Instantly his fingers closed, not harshly but with
gentle pressure she found reassuring.

"Nice talking with you, Mr. Kincaid," he said, and
drew her away.

"I can't believe you did that," Nora said when they
were back inside. The classical quartet had been replaced by a soft rock group. Couples were being drawn
out onto the dance floor in the center of the room. She
and Fletcher joined them.

He danced well, but she should have expected that
in a man who was so innately graceful. What she
hadn't expected—couldn't have—was the whole situation. Robert Kincaid might be one of nature's no-
blemen—or he might not—but either way he wasn't
going to be happy with what had just happened.

If that thought had occurred to Fletcher, it didn't
seem to bother him in any way. He gave her an almost
boyish grin and drew her closer against him.

"Did what?"

"You know perfectly well. You were rude to him."

"Oh, gosh, was I?"

"Fletcher—"

"It sure is tough for us backwoods types to put a
foot right in fancy society."

"Oh, please. You're as polished as anyone I've met.
I'm just saying you could have gone a little easier on
him, that's all."

"Why?" Fletcher asked quietly. "I got the distinct impression you weren't comfortable with the situation. If I was wrong, I apologize."

Nora took a breath. Being so close to him, moving to the music with his hand holding hers and his arm strong against her back, she was having trouble remembering anything Kincaid had said or done. Somehow it didn't seem important.

"No," she said softly, "you weren't wrong."

His hand tightened just a little at the curve of her waist. The music swept them on.

And on. They danced for hours, heedless of the time, pausing only to catch their breaths and raid the buffet. The music was fast, it was slow, it didn't matter. Nora hadn't danced in years, and she was making up for lost time and discovering in the process what the right partner could mean.

He was so graceful, this big, hard man with the crystal eyes. He held her gently, guided her easily, laughed and talked and smiled so that she lost all sense of time passing, all sense of place, even—truth be told—of herself.

With him, she felt like someone else. A self she had never met before. Carefree, a little reckless. Happy. Above all, happy.

Not that she hadn't been happy before, but this was different. It wasn't so much the satisfaction and contentment she had thought of as happiness. It was brighter, hotter, more real, more enticing.

And definitely irresistible. On that star-strewn spring night in the extravagantly luxurious house by the sea it was possible to forget everything else. Day would come soon enough and with it memory and responsibility.

But for the moment she delighted in being this woman she had never met before, this dancing, laughing, absurdly happy woman.

Only once, whirling in Fletcher's arms, did she happen to notice Robert Kincaid, see him standing off to one side, the good host observing his guests. Their eyes met for an instant. He smiled and lifted his glass in salute. But his gaze, what little she caught of it, was shuttered, hiding thoughts she couldn't guess at.

She forgot them instead and danced on until finally, how much time later she couldn't have said, she and Fletcher were out on the terrace, cooled by a gentle sea breeze, out of breath, senses whirling.

Fletcher laughed. He held her hand, looked into her eyes and said, "Let's blow this joint."

Her first impulse was regret; she didn't want the night to end. But then she felt the electricity in his touch and realized it had only begun.

In the Jeep, the house fading behind them, he asked, "Are you up for something different?"

"I guess—"

"Really different?"

Some other woman was cautious and deliberate. Some person she'd left behind would have thought of all the reasons to say no. Nora couldn't think of any.

She tipped her head back against the seat, closed her eyes and said, "Heck, why not."

"Great, I know just the place."

She felt him take a corner, changing direction and head north, away from the beach road.

Chapter 14

"Four ball in the corner pocket," Fletcher said.

You wouldn't think evening trousers would fit that well. Or that a man would look quite so good with his jacket discarded, tie gone and shirt unbuttoned at the collar. And the hair, that glorious leonine hair, just ruffled enough to make her fingers itch to smooth it.

Nora took a tighter grip on the cue she was holding and dragged her attention back to the table.

Plonk. The four ball disappeared. Fletcher straightened, walked around to the other side and thought for a moment. "Six ball in the side pocket."

He leaned forward, angled the cue, shot...and missed. Straightening again, he smiled. "Your turn."

Turn? Oh, right, the game. She glanced at the table, chalked the cue and—

"Six ball in the corner."

Fletcher's eyebrows rose but he said nothing, only stepped back politely. She'd missed her first shot, giving him the table, but she put that down to not having played in more years than she cared to remember. She had her bearings now.

Plonk.

"Seven ball in the side."

Plonk.

All those afternoons and evenings hanging out at all those army-run youth centers intended to keep kids like herself off foreign streets. All those wholesome hours spent studying the geometry of the pool table had had an effect, after all.

"Nine ball the hard way."

Plonk.

"Is there something about your misspent youth you haven't told me?" Fletcher asked. He looked mildly bemused.

Nora laughed. She was feeling good, really good, lighter somehow, as though her feet were no longer in contact with the ground.

"Lots of stuff," she said, and chalked the cue again.

He was a good loser. None of that macho, win-or-die business. To prove it, he bought the drinks. They sat at a table set back in a corner of the big, boisterous room decorated in pinks and greens straight out of the fifties. Vintage rock played, the tables were busy. Everybody seemed to be having a great time, this in spite—or maybe because—of the place being strictly no-alcohol.

"That's how they got the pool hall idea past the town fathers—and mothers," Fletcher explained as he refilled their glasses. Iced tea all the way. He stretched out in his chair, jacket tossed across the back of it, and took a long swallow.

Nora lowered her lashes to watch. She didn't do it consciously, it just happened. For a look-'em-straight-in-the-eye person, she was certainly discovering a whole new range of talents.

"So," he said as he put the glass down, "what were you doing when you weren't shooting pool?"

Nora hesitated. She'd never been inclined to talk much about herself. It just wasn't something she did and besides, most people weren't interested anyway.

"Just the usual," she replied. "School, sports, stuff like that."

"What about friends?"

She frowned slightly, surprised by his persistence. "We moved every year or so. It's hard to sustain friendships in that situation."

"Did your mom mind having to tear up so often?"

It was a leading question if ever she'd heard one. She had the distinct impression that he knew the answer—or at least suspected it—before she spoke.

"Mom bowed out early on. It was just Dad and me." Before he could say anything more, she added, "That happens. We managed fine."

"I wasn't going to suggest otherwise. But it still must have been rough."

"What about you, growing up in the city, yearning for the wide-open spaces? That couldn't have been fun."

"You're changing the subject," he said gently. "But that's your prerogative." He gestured toward the tables. "Want to play again?"

She should have said no. It was late, time to go, home to bed, to dream. Alone. But energy flowed through her and she didn't want the night to end.

"Sure," she replied and finished her drink.

This time he won. Not by much, it was a close game, but just by enough to make her laugh.

"Seems like I wasn't the only one with the misspent youth."

"There was a pool hall down the block from where I lived," he admitted. "It was run by this really weird old guy who had a back room full of stuffed birds and other animals. When I wasn't playing, I was in there looking at them."

"Didn't that give you the creeps, just a little?"

"Yeah, it did, but I kept thinking that if I watched them long enough, they'd move. Mostly it convinced me that I liked live animals a whole lot better than dead ones. The first time I saw a snowy owl actually fly across the sky, I thought it was the most beautiful sight ever."

"So all those hours in the pool hall were really responsible for making you the man you are today?"

He laughed. "Absolutely. The place burned down years ago, but I can still remember every inch of it, even the way it smelled, sawdust and beer, really dry old felt, guys coming in from what used to be called an honest day's work."

"Excuse me if I don't get all misty-eyed."

He put the cue down and smiled. "You know, someday I wouldn't mind seeing that."

"What?"

"You misty-eyed."

Nora didn't know what to say but she was spared the need by the clatter of chairs being turned over. "I think they're closing."

Fletcher nodded. They were among the few left. People were putting on their jackets, paying up.

"Night, folks," the man behind the counter said, voice fading behind the swinging doors.

They were outside on the sidewalk, the street rapidly emptying as people headed toward their cars. It wasn't far to the Jeep. The stores they walked past were shuttered, the movie theaters empty. The pool hall stayed open later than just about anywhere else.

"Nice evening," Fletcher said as he got in behind the wheel.

Nora nodded. She wasn't sure if he meant the weather or what they'd been doing, and she wasn't about to ask. It was safer that way.

"Tired?"

She'd had her eyes closed, head back against the seat, but now that he mentioned it she still felt all that strange, surging energy rushing through her.

"Not really."

"Me, neither. Hungry?"

"I can't be, not after what we ate at the party, but somehow I am."

"Hey, we got a lot of exercise. It was very aerobic."

"Must have been. Anyway, every place is closed."

"My place isn't."

"Oh, God, that's right, you cook."

"I'm not promising anything gourmet."

"Oh, well then, I'm not going."

"A little baked brie maybe, but that's it."

Baked brie. It was after midnight—well after—and the man was talking baked brie.

"What about grapes?"

"Okay, a few grapes."

"A little wine?"

"I could rustle up a decent Pouille Fuissy."

"You just do this sort of thing normally?"

"Absolutely...that and I thought maybe you'd end up coming over."

She turned her head, looking at him. "For the brie."

"Right, for the brie."

"Maybe a little espresso."

He glanced at her quickly before returning his eyes to the road. "What makes you think I do espresso?"

"What was that song in *The King and I*—'Getting to Know You'?"

"Great musical but *Showboat* was better."

"Not as good as *South Pacific*."

"You're kidding? You honestly think that?"

"Wouldn't anybody?"

"No, anybody wouldn't. *Showboat* is the greatest musical ever."

"You can't be serious. What about *Oklahoma?*"

"Not as good."

"I can't believe this," she said. "Okay, *Showboat* was terrific, but you can't seriously think it was better than *Oklahoma.*"

"I can, I do."

"Boy, you think you're getting to know someone and then you realize—"

"That they're as crazy about old musicals as you are?"

Nora laughed. "Yep. Okay, here's the clincher. What about *Carousel?*"

"You have to promise not to tell anyone."

"Pinky swear."

"The first time I saw it, I cried."

"You, too?"

He nodded. "I needed a tissue."

"I needed a dozen."

"You're a woman."

"Oh, no, you're not—?"

"What?"

"Sexist, one of the everything's-controlled-by-hormones bunch."

"I thought everything was controlled by the folks in the mother ship."

"Much better. What's your favorite sci-fi movie?"

"C'mon, that's not even hard, *The Day the Earth Stood Still.*"

"Not bad," she said. "But what about *Five Million Years to Earth?*"

"Oh, yeah! That was great. When they're digging down in that London subway and they find—"

This was getting dangerous. Really, truly, big-time dangerous. The guy made her laugh, sent her senses spinning and was interesting to talk with, too?

Maybe the espresso would clear her head.

Maybe she didn't want it cleared.

Maybe Gramma Liz had understood a whole lot more than she'd ever let on.

What time was it anyway? That time he'd talked about, between night and day, when everything seemed possible? Even laughter and dreams, and that last great shot she'd made spinning a three ball off the side, straight across the table, spinning and spinning—*plonk*—into the corner pocket.

If that could happen, absolutely anything could. She smiled, spinning down the road, through the night, back toward the endless, star-lit sea.

Chapter 15

"This is nice," Nora said. They were sitting in the main room of Fletcher's house in front of a fire. The structure was really more of a cabin—a first floor divided into living area, kitchenette and bath with a sleeping loft above.

Most of one wall was taken up by a worktable, including what looked like a state-of-the-art computer system and lab equipment. The floor was scrubbed pine with a couple of old, faded Persian rugs tossed across it. The furniture was earth-toned—an overstuffed couch, a few chairs. There was a table and four chairs that looked like they'd come from a farmhouse, bookshelves everywhere and several interesting pieces of folk art, wooden sculptures, painting, even a magnificent Amish quilt hanging above the fireplace.

The overall effect was comfortably casual, a place for an intelligent, confident man to live and work. Nora loved it. The only place she could remember seeing that she liked better was Amelia's house.

"Thanks," Fletcher said. He took the brie from the oven where it had warmed and cut several slices. Holding out one, he said, "Here, try this."

Without thinking, she leaned forward to take a bite of the tart, melted cheese surrounded by flaky pastry. The sensation was exquisite, a medley of flavors and textures that was practically sinful. Scratch that— definitely sinful. Being fed by him was a startlingly intimate experience. She drew back, flustered.

Fletcher busied himself pouring wine. A slight flush darkened his cheeks. He handed her a glass. "It's a warm night. Would you like to sit outside?"

She agreed at once, glad of anything that might mean more space between them. The house, delightful though it was, suddenly seemed too small.

Behind the house was a small shed and beyond it a backyard of rambling blackberry bushes and the wildflowers he had seeded running down to the beach. There was a battered picnic table with benches set near an old, gnarled fruit tree.

A sound came from the shed.

"What was that?" Nora asked, startled.

"My house guest." He set their glasses down. "Want to say hi?"

She nodded. Fletcher opened the shed door slightly. Nora leaned forward. She could hear the soft, whishing sound again and see something dark moving against the shadows.

"What is it?" she whispered.

"A gyrfalcon. I found her a week ago. She had a broken wing, but she's healing fast. I should be able to release her soon."

The falcon turned her head just then, giving Nora a glimpse of steel-bright eyes and a lethally curved beak.

"Do you take in many injured animals?" she asked as she drew back, closing the door carefully.

"Several times a year. The last one before this was a possum."

"What happened to it?"

"Got shot."

"What?"

"Fortunately it was only buckshot," he said as they walked back to the picnic table. They sat down together on a bench facing the distant, star-bright water. "It pulled through fine, but it'll be more careful whose garbage containers it tries to get into."

"I can't believe somebody would shoot at an animal just because it got into the garbage."

"People do all sorts of things," Fletcher said quietly. "You know that."

"I guess I do. It just seems as though in this place, with so much beauty and serenity, people ought to be better behaved."

"They are, for the most part. Did you notice how polite everyone was being tonight?"

"Where, at the pool hall?"

He laughed. "They're always polite there. I meant at the party. You could cut the ambition with a knife, not to mention the greed. But everyone was still on their best behavior."

"Because they kept their claws sheathed?"

"That counts. What did you think of Kincaid?"

Nora hesitated. She thought back to the scene on the terrace, her surprise that he should make his interest in her so obvious, and her suspicion about its source.

"He wasn't what I expected."

"How so?"

"I suppose I expected him to be more aloof."

"He looked real friendly to me."

"About that—"

"Look, I know I came on really hard but the way it looked—"

"Thanks."

He frowned slightly. "For what?"

"Stepping in the way you did. I was uncomfortable with the situation and I appreciate your help."

Fletcher laughed. He looked relieved. "Here I figured you'd think I was a real macho jerk."

"Listen, no guy who cooks the way you do can be a macho jerk."

"Really?"

"Cross my heart."

"I have other good points, too."

She took another sip of the wine. "You're kind to animals."

"That's true. But I was thinking along somewhat different lines."

She took a breath, slow, steady, perfumed with the night, and met his eyes. "Were you?"

He nodded, head bending gently, not rushing. She had plenty of time to withdraw, just move away, even a few inches. There wasn't a doubt in her mind that he would respect her feelings.

She stayed.

His mouth was firm and cool, tasting faintly of the wine. Her lips parted, savoring him, wanting more. He obliged, but only slightly, going very slowly. She felt the caution in him and the control, both holding back the passion. A part of her wished it wasn't so, but she understood his care, appreciated it. She had never desired a man as she did him, yet neither had she ever felt safer.

He drew back. She made a sound of protest and cupped his head. The kiss deepened, tongues teasing, bodies straining together. Caution slipped away. Nora stroked her hands down his broad back, feeling the strength and heat of him. She gasped as he drew her closer, her breasts straining against his rock-hard chest.

The night whispered around them, sea and stars the only reality. Boldly her tongue explored him, needing the taste and touch of this man who shattered all her safe, tidy preconceptions and made her sense how life could truly be.

They moved apart slightly, sharing quick, hungry kisses. She traced the curve of his jaw, the corded col-

umn of his throat, finding the hollow at the opening
of his shirt. The scent of him filled her, senses swim-
ming, reason fleeing. She moaned softly.

He drew a ragged breath, hands on her shoulders,
and gazed down into her eyes. "Nora...I don't want
you to regret anything. Hell, I don't want to regret
anything, either."

His smile was pained. "I can't believe I'm saying
this. You're all I've been able to think about. I've
never wanted a woman the way I do you but..."

"But it's all happening so fast," she said softly.

Fletcher nodded. "If I were younger...if I didn't
care so much—"

"If you were more of a boy and less of a man."

He touched her cheek gently with the back of his
hand. "Something like that."

Nora sighed, regret mingling with resignation. This
was no adolescent tit-for-tat for her doubts a few days
before. It was a sober and sensible assessment of their
situation. She should be glad of it.

And she was, really, or at least she would be when
her body quit hurting quite so much and her heartbeat stopped sounding like a kettledrum.

"I think I'd better take a rain check on the espresso," she murmured.

He drove her home, through the night and the quiet,
down the old beach road to the even older house. She
kept telling herself that she had done the right thing,
the mature thing. They both had. Too bad it felt so
wrong.

"Okay?" he asked softly when they had parked in front of Amelia's house. He was holding the door open for her, tall against the graying sky. That startled her.

"I hadn't realized," she said, getting out, not looking at him but so vividly aware all the same.

"What?"

"How late it is."

He glanced around, just realizing for himself. "You're right. Look."

She followed the direction he indicated out beyond the house, past the lawns, to the curve where land and water met and beyond, to where the sky was turning red.

Her smile was childlike, as sudden as sunlight after a storm. "I can't remember the last time I saw the dawn, except for after working all night, of course, and that shouldn't count."

"It doesn't," he said firmly. A moment passed, and then another. Abruptly, he reached down and took her hand. "Come on."

They kicked off their shoes at the edge of the trees and walked barefoot across the night-cool sand. Tiny waves lapped at them. Sandpipers darted back and forth, seeking an early breakfast. Gulls circled overhead, lazy, not quite awake yet.

And still the sun rose, banishing the night and all its shadows.

Nothing moved on the Sound. The earliest fishing boats had already gone out and none of the pleasure craft were stirring. The breeze flattened Nora's dress against her. It did the same to Fletcher's shirt and trousers, molding them to his body.

Neither spoke. It was a breathless time, carved out of reality and set apart. "See there," Fletcher said finally, pointing to a curve of the beach. "That's supposed to be where Amelia Daniels and the other settlers first came ashore."

"Is it really?"

"So legend has it."

"I'm surprised the family hasn't built a shrine of some sort, at least put up a plaque."

"There's been talk of that from time to time, but Liz wouldn't allow it."

"Why not? She was certainly proud of the family heritage."

"True, but she thought there'd already been enough of that sort of thing. She said it robbed the past of its humanity and made it irrelevant."

"She felt very strongly about that, didn't she?" Nora asked softly. "It wasn't just preserving a place that mattered to her. She wanted to keep it a part of the living world."

"I had a lot of respect for Liz, but what matters now is what you want."

Nora looked up at him. He stood with his back to the sun, dark against the fire-hued sky. Above his head, the last few stars were winking out.

Softly she said, "I really appreciated what you did back at your house."

His laugh was short and hard. "That's good because I can't remember the last time I had to really go to the mat with my conscience."

"Is that what you did?"

"Didn't you hear the thuds? Two out of three and I barely managed that."

"What would have happened if you'd lost?"

"I imagine that would have depended on you."

"Does it now?"

He went very still, watching her. She could see a pulse beating in his throat. "Be sure, Nora."

She was.

Chapter 16

She stood on tiptoe, pressing close all along the length of his body, her kiss hot and urgent. The male taste and scent of him overwhelmed her. She couldn't be close enough, couldn't have enough of him, know him enough.

He groaned deeply and wrapped his arms around her. His body was steel against the softness of her own. Without effort, he lifted her and mouths still clinging carried her up the beach toward the house.

When he had kicked the door closed behind them, he tore his mouth away long enough to utter a single word. "Where?"

The demand was hoarse, thick with desire. She drew breath, fought to comprehend, to think. "Upstairs."

Swiftly he mounted the steps. She was dimly aware of the hallway, a door opening, then light flooding through the windows facing the sea. But all of that was inconsequential compared to the hunger driving her, unlike any she had ever known.

It was all-consuming, this passion he made her feel, burning away every other consideration. Nothing mattered except the man who held her so powerfully.

He set her down lightly beside the four-poster bed heaped with lace-edged pillows and hung with richly embroidered curtains from another age, a sanctuary from the world.

His hands trembled as he traced the high curve of her breasts, spanning her narrow waist to the gentle swell of her hips and beyond. Gathering the skirt, he pulled it up, stroking her silk-sheathed thighs. She cried out softly, her palms braced against his chest.

"Fletcher, I don't know how much of this I can stand."

He smiled then, almost gently despite the fire gleaming in his eyes. "Let's find out, shall we?"

She shivered at the low, caressing tone of his voice, so like his touch, reassuring and possessive all at once. Cupping her buttocks, he moved her closer to him, making her vividly aware of his arousal. She gasped, her head falling back, and felt the room whirling around her.

When it stopped, she was lying on her back on the bed, staring up at Fletcher. He straddled her, a knee on either side, his weight braced on his arms. Her skirt was up around her waist. Slowly, watching her all the time, he slipped his fingers beneath the elastic of her panties and eased them down her legs.

It was a shocking act, coming so suddenly and unexpectedly. As cool air touched her, she gasped and instinctively tried to cover herself. But Fletcher caught both her wrists in one hand, raising them gently above her head. His mouth claimed hers, long and lingeringly, tongue driving deep.

Her back arched as liquid heat surged within her. She felt shameless, brazen and still—as he had demanded—so very sure. There was a rightness about this, almost a shock of recognition as though, unwittingly, she had been waiting for this man and this man alone. His slightest touch inflamed her, filling her with a need that was a kind of power in itself.

She moaned and tried to reach for him, but he restrained her tenderly. With his free hand, he cupped her breast through the lace-and-silk dress.

"This is a pretty thing," he said, touching the fabric lightly. "But please tell me it has a zipper."

Nora smiled. A giggle escaped her. "I'm afraid not, just buttons. I had the devil's own time getting them all fastened."

He sighed deeply, a man summoning all the patience of which he is capable and then some. Swiftly he turned her over. She lay facedown between his thighs as he rapidly undid the buttons. They were tiny and covered in silk, slippery to the touch.

Fletcher cursed, persevered, cursed again. At last he was rewarded when the last one slid free.

The bodice of the dress was constructed so that she had no need to wear a bra. When he slipped it from her, she was naked beneath him.

The blatant desire and approval in his gaze as he studied her made Nora tremble. Instinctively she reached for his shirt. "This isn't fair," she said. "I want you the same way."

"I hope so," he said as she began undoing the buttons as rapidly as he had undone hers. "Sweet heaven, I hope so."

The shirt fell open. He shrugged it off, revealing a massive chest and shoulders perfectly formed of granite-hard muscle. The power in him was so obvious that Nora bit down hard on her lower lip. He was everything she had ever imagined in a man and then some, even to the dusting of golden hair so teasingly soft beneath her fingertips.

The clasp of his evening trousers refused to yield at first. But she gave it a good, hard yank, causing him to laugh, and it opened. Hastily he stripped off his remaining clothes and came to her in glorious nature, unfettered by any restraints.

She fell back against the pillows, gazing at him. Softly, on a whisper of sound, she said, "You are so beautiful."

His smile was hard with desire kept barely in check. "I'm glad you think so but you are—beyond anything. I want to go so slowly with you—"

"Not too slowly," she said, sliding her hands down over his rock-firm abdomen and gently cupping his manhood.

He gasped and jerked as though a shock had struck him. Gracefully she drew herself upright so that she was kneeling before him and lowered her head, blowing lightly on his fully erect member. "Beautiful," she murmured.

Hard hands grasped her, lowering her onto the bed. A powerful thigh surged between her own. "Next time," he said, voice rasping, "next time will be slower."

His mouth closed on her nipples, first one, then the other, tugging urgently. She almost surged off the bed, so intense was her response. He held her, moving down her body, laving lightly at her navel. Fingers slipped along her petal-smooth inner thighs, finding the heat and dampness of her, opening her gently.

She cried out, straining for him. He slipped a finger into her, withdrew, returned, stretching her. "You're so tight," he said, almost harshly, his control all but exhausted.

Her fingers clawed at his broad back, hips rising. "I want you so much, please—"

Her entreaty seemed to convince him. He uttered a thick sound that might have been her name and surged against her. Yet even as he brought them together, his control seemed to reassert itself. He went slowly, entering her only the smallest amount, giving her time to become accustomed before thrusting slowly and deeply.

Her eyes opened wide at the sensation, so extraordinarily powerful and demanding. She was no longer merely herself but more, part of him, taken by him and taking. His face was tautly drawn, eyes blue fire, as he withdrew with excruciating care, almost leaving her before returning even deeper than before.

And so he continued, thrusting hard and slow. Sweat dampened his back, his features were rigid. He was trembling with the force of his own need, but not yet willing to surrender to it.

Spiraling tension built in her, drawing tighter and tighter. She cried out, stunned by the force of it. Tidal waves of pleasure exploded throughout her.

He groaned, triumphant, and shuddered in her arms.

Nora woke to sunlight pouring in through the windows. She was lying on her side so that her first sight upon opening her eyes was the man beside her. He slept deeply, lashes shadowing his cheeks, his breathing deep and regular.

She stared at him for a long moment, feeling the lingering echoes of pleasure deep within her. Astonishment at what had happened heightened every memory, endowing it with startling clarity.

But beyond that was tenderness, uncurling with every breath she took, like a flower opening to the sun. Great, boundless tenderness for this man, this friend, this lover.

She got up carefully, anxious not to disturb him. Recovering their clothes from where they had been abandoned on the floor, she hung them over the back of a chair, then plucked her robe from the bathroom door.

With the robe wrapped around her, she went downstairs. The aching awareness of her body brought a smile. There was no discomfort to it, only a new and rather fierce sensitivity, as though she was more alive than she had ever been.

Entering the kitchen, she noticed that shapes and colors seemed sharper somehow, more vivid. She was even more conscious of the mingling smells of the old house—herbs and beeswax, brick and wood and the ever-present sea.

Running water into the coffeemaker, she happened to glance at her computer. The little screen was blank and uninviting. She felt no particular urge to switch it back on, but knew she would have to eventually. There were still far too many unanswered questions about Kincaid Industries, actually more now that she'd met Robert Kincaid. But for once in her life, work would have to wait.

She decided to cook. The urge, so novel to her, was so intense that she laughed. Obviously Fletcher had awakened all sorts of womanly instincts. She only had to hope he could withstand the consequences.

Lacking a microwave, she was momentarily stumped. But then she remembered that all sorts of things could be cooked on an ordinary stove. Bacon and eggs, for instance, so simple that she was convinced not even she could wreck them.

Her confidence proved well-founded. She had bacon crisping nicely in a skillet and eggs waiting to be scrambled, fresh orange juice squeezed and the coffee ready when the phone rang.

Nora got it on the second ring, hoping Fletcher hadn't been awakened. She wanted to surprise him in bed with the results of her efforts.

"Miss Delaney?" a familiar voice asked.

"Mr. Sanders." Her voice held a note of surprise. It was Sunday after all, not a time she'd normally expect to hear from the lawyer.

"I was hoping I wouldn't have to bother you again so soon but it looks as though Charlotte Delaney isn't prepared to be patient much longer."

Nora's hand tightened on the receiver. "Oh, really? I'm sorry to hear that."

"So was I. She wants to know your plans."

"She isn't the only one."

"What's that?"

"Sorry, I was just thinking out loud."

She would love to know for herself what she intended, but the moment she tried to think seriously about the future, she felt only confusion and a certain degree of fear. Everything was changing so quickly. The temptation to live for the moment and not worry about any consequences was overwhelming.

"I really don't think Charlotte has any right to try to pressure me into making a decision," Nora said firmly.

"Maybe you'd better tell her that. She doesn't seem to believe it coming from me."

"Maybe I'd better. I'll call—"

"Actually," the young attorney interrupted, "Miss Charlotte has called a family meeting for this afternoon at these offices."

Nora's eyes widened. "This afternoon?"

"That's right. In three hours."

"Just like that?"

"Let's say we've had a long-standing relationship with the family that inclines us to be more accommodating than we might be otherwise."

"You mean she browbeat you into it?"

"Something like that. At any rate, it's easy to see what she's doing. By having the meeting here, she gives the impression of being on neutral ground, but at the same time she can rally the family to proceed against you."

"As in challenge the will?"

"It could come to that," he admitted.

"Only if she's prepared to get up in court and declare that Gramma Liz was mentally incompetent. Will she go that far?"

"It's hard to know with Charlotte," Sanders said. "But once she's got the bit between her teeth, it's damned hard to dislodge."

"I see . . ." Nora took a deep breath, struggling for calm. She deeply resented what her relative was doing, largely because it intruded on the fragile sense of happiness that had been growing within her.

"Does Charlotte know you're calling me?"

"I believe I overlooked mentioning that in my conversation with her."

"Good," Nora said. At least she would have surprise on her side. "Three hours. I'll be there."

She hung the phone up, but stood looking at it for a moment as she tried to get her thoughts in order. Charlotte's position was obvious—she wanted Amelia's house for the family and she would do basically anything she had to in order to get it.

Against that, what did Nora want? It was a straightforward question, one the family had a right to ask. She simply wasn't prepared to answer it yet.

She shook her head slightly, astonished at her own confusion. Scant days before, Gramma Liz's will had made as little sense to her as it did to everyone else. The idea of staying on in the house was still completely impractical. She had her life, her career, her responsibilities. And besides, she wasn't a country person.

Yet, gazing out the kitchen window at the old oak tree where the owls lived, she felt a tug of yearning so intense that it stole her breath away. It was as though the house and everything to do with it was slowly but surely changing her. Within its walls, she was becoming someone different.

But the house alone was certainly not responsible. Far more credit—or blame—had to be given to Nora herself and what she felt for the proud, gentle man asleep in her bed.

With a wry smile, she set the bacon to drain and quickly scrambled the eggs. Three hours, Sanders had said. Getting a tray from the cupboard, she resolved to make the most of them.

Chapter 17

"Are you sure you don't want me to come?" Fletcher asked.

They were seated at the kitchen table, eating warmed over scrambled eggs and bacon. The sun was considerably higher than it had been when the food was first cooked, but neither gave any sign of minding. Languorous relaxation filled Nora, dented only slightly by the coming confrontation with Charlotte.

"I'd love for you to," she admitted, "but I think I have to handle this by myself. Besides, you can't honestly tell me you want to be involved?"

"Not particularly," he agreed. "Family squabbles are always unpleasant. I just don't want you to be ganged up on."

"But I'll have Sanders there," she said, eyes teasing.

Fletcher laughed. "He's a nice guy, but don't expect him to go head-to-head with Charlotte."

"Too tough for him?"

"Too used to getting her own way. Liz could handle her, though."

"I figured she must have since she didn't write the will Charlotte obviously expected. Do you have any idea what Gramma's secret was?"

Fletcher took another swallow of his coffee and put the cup down before answering. "She always impressed me as someone with a very clear vision of how she wanted her life to be. I don't mean to suggest that she was at all self-centered, she wasn't. But she had great inner strength and powerful values. Together, they guided her."

"She was lucky," Nora said quietly. "Too many people fumble their way through life. They never really seize hold of it and make something that's uniquely their own."

"Liz sure did and in her own way, Charlotte isn't all that different. She just comes at if from another direction." He looked at Nora perceptively. "When all's said and done, I suspect you have a lot in common with the women of your family."

"Maybe so, but I don't expect to find much common ground with Charlotte. She's high-handed and presumptuous. The fact is I don't much like her."

"You're not required to," Fletcher reminded her gently. "But remember, there'll be other people at the meeting. As used as they are to being led by Charlotte, it's possible you might find some allies."

"I hope so," Nora said and only then realized how desperately she meant it. "Except for Dad and Gramma Liz, I don't have much experience with families."

"Don't worry about that. The Delaneys and ancillary branches are really much more than a family. They're more like a clan than anything else."

"Oh, great," Nora muttered. "A nice, big, complicated clan all of whom think I have no business being here. I feel so much better knowing that."

Fletcher pushed back from the table. He wore the evening trousers he'd had on the previous night but his chest was bare. Nora remembered how the taut covering of downy soft curls over rock-hard muscle felt against her cheek and shivered inwardly.

"I wouldn't be so sure about what the others think," he said as he stood up and came around to where she was sitting. Gently he brushed her cheek, his fingers drifting into her hair to stroke the short, auburn strands. "I wouldn't care so much, either."

"Easy for you to say," she murmured. Her chest felt tight. Astonishingly she yearned for him again already. He made her ache with longing and with a vulnerability that frightened her.

"Not easy," he corrected and touched his mouth lightly to hers. "Everything seems more complicated suddenly."

She managed a wan smile. "You, too? That's reassuring, at least."

He kissed her again with great gentleness, then stepped back. "You'd better get ready."

Since she was wearing nothing but his shirt that seemed like good advice. By the time she had showered and dressed in conservatively cut slacks and a lightweight sweater, she was feeling less nervous.

Fletcher was in the bedroom when she came back out. He was tucking the shirt back into his trousers. Her equanimity crumbled just a bit when he smiled and said, "It smells of you now, all sunshine and roses."

"Is that what I smell like?" Not printouts and adding machine paper, day-old coffee and yellow highlighter?

"Roses," he confirmed, "the small wild ones that grow down by the beach in high summer."

Oh, those. She remembered sticking her nose into them one time, city child stunned by the sensations of the country. The scent wasn't as sweet as tame, domesticated roses. It had a hint of a bite to it.

"And sunshine," he repeated. "Hot noon sun, the kind that can make a man think he could die of thirst."

"You can be very distracting, you know."

His eyes crinkled. "Can I?"

"I've always tried to avoid distractions."

"Kept your mind on business?"

"Eye on the ball."

"Nose to the grindstone?"

"Head in the sand, whatever." She took a breath, and let it out slowly. It didn't help. Her heart was racing and she felt light-headed, all for reasons that had nothing at all to do with Charlotte Delaney and her dumb, stupid, badly timed meeting.

"I'd better go."

"I'll walk out with you."

"By the way," she said as they shut the door. "How are the owls doing?"

"Fine. Mom and Dad are working hard, and the kids are growing fast. Nature's taking it course."

"Like it always does?"

He nodded. "Seems to." Without warning, he wrapped a steely arm around her waist and pulled her hard against him. His kiss was swift, thorough and devastating.

When he raised his head, his eyes glittered like shards of blue ice. "Give 'em hell, sweetheart. And remember, you're the one Liz picked. In the final analysis, it's not what they want that matters. It's what you want."

He made it sound so simple. They both knew it wasn't.

Where the road to Daniels' Neck met the beach road, they parted. Fletcher headed back to his cabin while Nora turned north toward town. The day was clear and warm. She had the windows down and could smell the sea. It was a far cry from the world as she had known it—filled with the sounds and sights and odors of the city. A far cry, indeed.

But it could be her world, if she wanted it to be.

All she had to do was stand up to the clan, face Charlotte and follow the dictates of her heart.

The first two she could do, no problem. It was the last one that had her well and truly stumped.

But fortunately, she reminded herself, no one at Jerome Sanders's office would know that.

She took it as a good omen when she found a parking spot almost directly in front of the law offices. Even on Sunday, the main street of Belle Haven was a busy place. Since the blue laws had been done away with, most people seized the opportunity to shop. She skirted around a mother with two small children, avoided bumping into a gaggle of teenagers and went into the building.

The offices were up a short flight of stairs. By New York standards, they weren't particularly plush. But they did have the settled, comfortable air of a well-established firm built on serving the same community—and the same families—for generations.

Jerome was in the reception area. She got the impression that he had been lingering there to catch her. He gave her a quick, nervous smile.

"They're all here."

Nora raised her eyebrows. "All?" She glanced through the glass doors toward the offices.

"All the heavyweights, anyway. Every branch of the family seems to be represented. I may as well tell you, they look as though they've come loaded for bear."

Her stomach clenched, but nothing in her expression revealed it. She lifted her head, gave Sanders a serene smile and said, "Then I suggest we get started."

Chapter 18

"We simply want to know what you intend," Charlotte Delaney said. "Surely, there is nothing unreasonable about that."

Nora kept her face expressionless. They were barely fifteen minutes into the meeting and she was having a hard time resisting the urge to take Charlotte down a peg or two. The woman was overbearing, self-centered and opinionated in the extreme. She seemed to think that when she said jump all Nora should ask was how high.

Obviously Charlotte had not survived in the world of major accounting firms, where the lure of partnerships caused otherwise sane people to do remarkable things. Nor had she gone head-to-head with some of the most aggressive—and sometimes felonious—business executives in the country.

Nora had, although she had never before quite so appreciated what that experience meant for her. "Excuse me," she said with excruciating courtesy, "but please help me to understand. When we last spoke, you accused me of having coerced Grandmother into changing her will in my favor and suggested that you meant to challenge it. Am I to understand that now your sole interest is in determining my intentions?"

There was a stir throughout the room. Some dozen members of the family had turned out for the event. Most were known to Nora at least vaguely; their faces looked familiar. A few were complete strangers, but bore the stamp of shared family features.

Jerome had made the introductions. They were a mix of Delaneys, Marlowes and Nashes, representing the different branches of the family that had developed since the founding. So far, the six men and a like number of women seemed to be content to let Charlotte do the talking.

But now, presented with Nora's challenge, they sat up and took notice. A little white-haired lady who had been presented as Martha Nash smiled at Nora.

"Why the girl's got spunk, Harold. Listen to her."

The younger man—which was to say seventy rather than ninety—seated beside the lady bobbed his head up and down approvingly. "Sounds like maybe Charlotte's bit off more than she can chew," he said with obvious satisfaction.

"We'll see about that," Charlotte muttered. "If you want a fight on your hands, you'll have it," she told Nora stiffly. "I stand by what I said to you, Elizabeth would never have left Amelia's house to you if she'd been in her right mind."

"How would you know whether she was or not?" Nora demanded. "Or are you claiming to have been especially close to her?"

Charlotte's cheeks pinked. "Of course I was. We were family, after all. Unlike you, I've lived all my life in Belle Haven."

"But not at Amelia's house." Martha Nash chimed in. "As I recall, you weren't all that frequent a visitor there, especially not after you and Lizzie had the falling out over that silly plaque."

Nora listened attentively. Fletcher had said something about Gramma Liz refusing to allow a plaque to be put up on the beach. "The one you wanted to put up where the first settlers came ashore?"

Charlotte looked startled. "You know about that?"

"I know about a lot of things, including the fact that Gramma Liz never wanted the house turned into a museum. She believed it should be lived in just as it always had been."

"Liz had no appreciation of the historical significance of the property," Charlotte said. "She treated it as though it was the most ordinary of homes. Why she installed cable!"

Nora laughed. She couldn't help it. "How terrible. Why in another few years she would probably have put in a satellite dish or wired the place for fiber optics.''

''It's not a joke,'' Charlotte insisted. ''Amelia's house is a priceless historical legacy. It should be restored to exactly the way it was.''

''Why? So no one can live there anymore and all the life goes out of the place?''

''So it can be properly respected and, yes, revered. You have no idea of the sacrifices our ancestors made, the enormous trials they overcame. The house should be a shrine to them, a place where people can go—the right people, of course—to remember how we came to be.''

''A shrine?'' Nora repeated, dumbfounded. She could just imagine what Gramma Liz would have said to that. ''It's a home where people lived, children were born, pets were kept, there was laughter and tears and plenty of messes. It's not some awful, dead shrine!''

''Give it to her, girl.'' Martha chortled. ''She had us all thinking you were going to sell it to some damn developer, but it seems like you've got more feeling for the place than anybody else. Maybe Liz wasn't so crazy after all.''

''She wasn't crazy period,'' said a voice from the door.

Nora whirled around. So did everyone else. They stared at a tall, silver-haired man with a sailor's tan and a devilish grin. He was certainly beyond sixty, possibly even into his seventies, but there was no denying that he possessed a certain roguish charm. Even Nora wasn't entirely immune to it.

"Patrick Delaney," he said and came forward to clasp her hand in his.

"You're . . . it's your book I've been reading."

He looked pleased. "That thing? Good God, why does anybody keep it around?"

"It's a wonderful book," Nora said. "I'm enjoying it tremendously."

He released her hand, but pulled up a chair so that he could sit close to her. "Well, now, I suppose it does have a few merits. What part are you up to?"

"The 1890s, when Brand Delaney came up from New York to build a house near Daniels' Neck."

"And met prim-and-proper Miss Julia Nash."

Nora laughed. "Who promptly turned into not-so-prim-and- proper."

"Boy, did she ever. Folks are still talking about that."

"No, they are not," Charlotte said, interrupting. She shot Patrick Delaney a look that would have shriveled another man. He stared back impassively except for the small smile playing at his mouth.

"Brand Delaney was my grandfather," he said. "Your father's, too, though through another son. He and Julia had four sons altogether and two daughters. He never did build his grand house, but the way I heard it, he never regretted that."

"He did, however, add the land he had bought to Julia's own, thereby extending the holding," Charlotte said. "Even though he was an outsider, he protected Amelia's house and all it stood for."

"I don't think Brand Delaney ever gave a thought to that house standing for anything," Patrick said. "It was a home, a place for loving—and living. You don't want to admit that, Charlotte. Somehow, you've never understood it. But Liz did."

He looked at Nora. "You never asked her for it, did you?"

"No," she said softly. "Of course not."

"And when you found out she'd left it to you, you were flabbergasted."

"Stunned."

"That's what I figured. How can anyone expect you to know what you want to do with the place when you haven't had any chance to get used to it being yours? If you take my advice, Nora Delaney, you'll make sure you get that chance. This is too big a decision to make in a rush."

Charlotte jumped up. Her thin face was flushed and her hands were clenched. "Be quiet, Patrick. You have no idea what you're talking about. We can't possibly take the risk that she'll sell to outsiders. She has to agree now to keep the property within the family."

Turning to Nora, she said, "Perhaps we can't afford to pay what someone would who was going to clear the land and build a dozen of those horrible McMansions, but we're hardly poor. We can reimburse you very nicely. You'll be a rich woman. You can go anywhere you like, do anything you want. Surely that matters more than a house you say you never wanted in the first place?"

Surely it did. Didn't it?

She liked her work well enough, but the thought of the freedom such money would bring was undeniably tempting. She could travel anywhere, see the world, be completely footloose. For someone who had never had roots and never wanted them, that should be ideal.

Shouldn't it?

Nora stood up. She put on her best impassive gaze, glanced at Charlotte, then deliberately turned to Jerome Sanders. He was the lawyer, after all, the professional who was supposed to make sense of the tangles people got themselves into.

Quietly she said, "I'll think it over."

Without further word, she walked toward the door.

Charlotte raised her voice. "That's it? You'll think it over? That's all you have to say?"

Patrick put a hand to her shoulder. He stared at Nora thoughtfully. "Down, Charlotte. You've said your piece. You'll get your answer when she's ready."

"It's not *my* answer, you oaf. I'm doing this for the family. She's not really a part of it, never has been. She has no right—"

"That's enough," Patrick said. His voice sliced through the room. For just a moment, Nora thought she caught a glimpse of how his grandfather might have been, the bold robber baron who had swept Miss Julia Nash off her feet.

Martha Nash was smiling, as was her son. Come to think of it, several other members of the family were looking pleased. There was an air of excitement in the room, as though she had surprised them in a way they didn't at all mind.

"I'll be in touch," Nora said, more gently this time, and went out the door.

She sat in the car for several minutes before starting it. The scene in the law office kept running through her mind. Charlotte was angry and determined, there was no getting around that. But the others had been a surprise. They seemed much more inclined to accept her than she had thought.

But then, they were her family. She'd never really thought much about that but it was true. These people who were still largely strangers to her were also bound to her in ways she was just beginning to sense.

If she stayed, they would be there, all these hitherto unknown aunts and uncles, cousins, in-laws, nieces and nephews. The people who had never been a part of her life yet to whom she was undeniably tied. The thought was daunting yet not without a certain appeal.

She had never really belonged anywhere except in the professional niche she'd made for herself. Even that was transient; witness how she moved from client to client, towing her little computer and parking herself wherever she had to.

If she stayed, all that would change.

She would be committing herself to something she had never experienced and barely understood.

And that was without even mentioning Fletcher.

At the mere thought of him, her body tightened. The yearning that filled her was so intense she could barely breathe.

The door to the law office opened; others were coming out. She didn't want them to see her like this, vulnerable and confused. Quickly she started the car and pulled into traffic.

Chapter 19

Nora was home, making a pot of tea, when the phone rang. It was Kincaid. Once the pleasantries were out of the way, he got right to the point.

"We didn't have much chance to get acquainted last night. How about coming out on the boat for lunch?"

No chance he was talking about a modest sailboat. This might be the only time in her life that she was invited on board a genuine yacht complete with a handsome multimillionaire.

"Gosh, I'd love to, but I'm afraid I've already made plans."

Silence. Clearly Robert Kincaid was not accustomed to people saying no to him.

"Can't you change them?"

Sure she could. The problem was she didn't want to. She preferred to stay home, bury herself in work and try not to wonder when Fletcher would call. If he called, was an entirely different matter that she refused to think about at all.

"It would be terribly difficult. I'm sure you understand. Thanks awfully for thinking of me. Oh, and I did have a wonderful time last night. Your house is magnificent."

That seemed to cheer him up, if only marginally. He still sounded just a bit like a petulant boy, startled to discover that he couldn't always have his own way.

Perverse as the male of the species could be, that only seemed to increase his interest. "I'll call you tomorrow," he said. "We really should get together. After all, we're neighbors."

Nora hung up, puzzling over the call. She was still no closer to knowing whether it was her land Robert Kincaid wanted or her complicity in the audit of his company.

The possibility that he was genuinely attracted to her flitted through her mind briefly but she dismissed it. She simply could not see a man used to having people—especially women—fawn over him being drawn to someone as independent as herself.

Neither could she envision two men as different from one another as Fletcher and Kincaid being attracted to the same woman.

But then she had never claimed to understand much about men. In light of recent events, she probably understood even less than she'd thought.

Numbers, however, were another matter. She understood them extremely well. Tea in hand, she sat down at the computer and prepared to immerse herself once again in the tangled web of Kincaid Industries.

The task was made more difficult by her mind's tendency to wander off in different directions, all of them somehow leading to Fletcher. But she persevered, getting up only to refill her teacup and stretch the kinks out of her shoulders.

The spring afternoon drifted toward evening. Nora did her best to ignore the fact that the phone hadn't rung again and kept working. Several hours into it, just when her head was beginning to ache, she began following a stray strand down through the layers of transactions, searching a vague memory that was beginning to surface.

She was tracing yet another of Kincaid's subsidiary companies, trying to remember where else she'd encountered the name when it suddenly came to her. The company was one of those involved in so many of the transactions below the legal reporting limit. But this one seemed larger than the others and more active.

It was also based, so far as she could tell, offshore. That by itself didn't necessarily mean anything, but it kept her interest high. She continued following it until, abruptly, she hit a blank wall. The company disappeared beneath the layers of subsidiaries, joint ownerships, partnerships, sole proprietorships and the like that she was just beginning to realize were the real heart of Kincaid Industries.

She rubbed the back of her neck and stared at the screen. Why on earth would anyone create such a Byzantine web of organizations if not to conceal information? But what information and why? Was Robert Kincaid involved in actual criminal activity or was he merely a canny businessman who liked to keep as much hidden from his competitors as possible?

The truth was that she had no idea, but experience had taught her to suspect the worst. Before she was done, she would know it.

Her head really was throbbing. She got up and went over to the sink, running cold water on a paper towel and holding it over her eyes. As she did so, the phone rang.

After so many hours of silence, the sound seemed to bounce off the walls. Nora grabbed for the receiver.

"I'm sorry I didn't call sooner," Fletcher said. "Somebody dropped off a sick opossum on my doorstep and I had to take him to the vet. How did the meeting go?"

"Fine," Nora said. She had a sudden impulse to laugh, but managed to control it. Of all the excuses she'd ever heard, having to take care of a sick opossum definitely got top marks.

"How's the patient?"

"He's got a broken rear leg. Looks like he might have been hit by a car, but he'll mend. So did Charlotte do her barracuda act?"

"She tried to, but a funny thing happened. I got the impression some of the other members of the family weren't all that firmly behind her. When I said I needed more time, they didn't object. Oh, and Patrick Delaney was there. He was great.''

''No kidding.''

The deadpan way he said that, with a tiny note of satisfaction, alerted her. ''Didn't you say the two of you go fishing sometimes?''

''We've been known to.''

''You wouldn't have happened to let him know about the meeting, would you?''

''Now why would you think that?''

''Because it just occurred to me that Charlotte probably wouldn't have asked him herself.''

''Then he must have gotten wind of it somehow.''

''Fletcher—''

''Are you sorry he was there?''

''No, but I'm a big girl. I'm supposed to fight my own battles.''

''You did fight it. I'm sure you were great.''

''How sure?''

''You were, weren't you?''

''I was satisfied with the outcome,'' she said cautiously. ''What did you do, check in with Patrick?''

''I ran into him outside the vet's,'' Fletcher admitted. He sounded chagrined that she'd discovered what he'd done. ''He was singing your praises, by the way. Says you're the best thing that's happened in the family in years.''

''Could that have anything to do with my telling him how much I like his book?''

''Maybe a touch. Seriously, I'm glad it went well.''

His concern warmed her. She was so unused to having anyone even know when she had some problem, much less care about the outcome. Softly she said, "I miss you."

There was silence for a moment before he said, "That can be remedied."

"You won't be sitting up with a sick opossum?"

"I think he'd rather be alone."

"I wouldn't."

She held her breath, waiting to hear what he'd say. His response didn't disappoint her.

"Five minutes." The phone clicked off.

Five minutes? What was she supposed to do with that? Shut down the computer, tidy up the kitchen, race upstairs, pull off the clothes she'd worn to the meeting and throw on something a little more—romantic? Seductive? Fun?

Her wardrobe didn't exactly run to that. With the exception of the dress she'd worn the previous night, her clothes tended to be ovewhelmingly practical. Or at least, the clothes she showed to the world.

Delving into a drawer, she emerged holding a lace teddy. Beautiful, sensuous lingerie could be an expensive habit, but it was one she was glad she'd acquired. On top, she tossed a thin cotton knit skirt normally worn at a sedate length but when the waistband was folded over several more times it revealed a good deal more leg. Lastly she grabbed a neatly ironed and starched business shirt, left most of the buttons undone and tied the ends around her waist.

As outfits went, it wasn't great, but it was a far cry from her usual and that was exactly what she wanted. Racing back down the stairs, she got there just as Fletcher knocked on the kitchen door.

She took a deep breath, pinned on a smile and opened it."

"Hi."

Sweet heaven, he looked good, standing there in jeans and a pullover, looking straight back at her. His hair was slightly mussed by the wind. There was a tiny cut on one corner of his chin where he'd nicked himself shaving.

Without thought, she raised herself slightly and pressed her lips to the cut. He breathed in sharply, his arms wrapping around her.

"You feel so good," he said.

"You, too," she murmured, so very, very glad that he was there, warm and solid, just as she remembered. Glad, most of all, that there were no regrets, only pure, simple joy at being with him again.

They went inside. Fletcher still had his arms around her. Her feet weren't quite touching the floor. Nora laughed. Trade all this for lunch on a yacht with a millionaire? She'd have to be crazy.

"We could sit down and talk," Fletcher said.

"Or watch TV," she suggested, smiling.

"Play cards."

"Do hat tricks."

"Or we could—"

"Oh, yes, please," she murmured and kissed him hotly.

They made it to the bedroom, just barely. Fletcher fumbled with the ties of her shirt, but they yielded quickly. He pulled it off, kissing her urgently, and urged her back toward the bed.

She clung to him, her hands beneath his sweater, stroking his powerfully muscled back. Desire surged through her, making her shake with the force of it.

Her skirt fell away, leaving her in the teddy of apricot silk tipped with tea-hued lace. When Fletcher saw it, his eyes narrowed. "What's this?" he murmured, fingering the fragile material.

"My secret vice," she whispered and lightly nibbled at his lower lip.

The effect was most gratifying. He made a hard sound deep in his throat and stripped his jeans off with fierce efficiency. His big hands, the palms callused from all the outdoor work he did, cupped her breasts. Lightly, with great control, he rubbed his thumbs over her nipples.

Nora shut her eyes for a moment against the crescendo of sensations surging through her. Instinctively she clung to him as the only solidness in a world rocking to its foundations.

He lifted her high against him and laid her gently on the bed, coming down swiftly to cover her. His mouth and hands pushed the teddy away, his tongue stroking every inch of her skin as it was revealed.

Thickly he murmured, "You taste like honey."

Nora barely heard him. Gasping, she trailed her fingertips over his chest, down across his flat abdomen to stroke his manhood. He groaned and moved suddenly, reversing their positions so that he was on his back and she was above him.

"I wanted to wait," he said between clenched teeth. "I swear I did."

A heady sense of power surged through Nora. Slowly, teasingly, she lowered herself onto him. His hands grasped her hips, but he made no attempt to control her, letting her set the pace.

The tip of her tongue touched her lips. Her eyelids dropped, heavy with languor. Carefully, exercising all the control she could muster, she began to move. Her breath was ragged and a fine sheen of perspiration glistened over her skin. Each stroke brought him deeper into her, filling her completely.

He slipped a hand between them, stroking the tiny nub nestled within damp curls. Unbearable tension coiled within her, winding tighter and tighter until she could bear no more.

Nora screamed. Her release was shattering. Even as it came, Fletcher took control, surging into her, driving hard and deep to his own completion.

Chapter 20

"Not like that," Fletcher said.

Nora paused and looked at him quizzically. "No?"

He shook his head. Putting his hand over hers, he guided her. "Like this."

She pulled, slowly but firmly, and was rewarded when a particularly intransigent weed finally yielded. Pleased, she tossed it away and reached for the next one.

They were in the garden behind the house. It was late morning. Fletcher had stayed overnight with the result that they'd gotten little sleep. Neither minded. The day was clear, the breeze downright balmy. The garden smelled of fertile earth and burgeoning life. Nora loved it.

"This is great," she said. "How come no one ever told me pulling weeds was a great stress reliever?"

"You think this is good, you should try laying brick. Now that really gets rid of stress."

"Thanks, but I think I'll stick to weeding." She sat back on her haunches and looked around with an air of satisfaction. They'd been working little more than an hour, but already Amelia's garden—as it had always been called—was looking better. Tiny green shoots were inching their way out of the rich dark earth everywhere she looked.

"Do you have any idea what these are?" she asked, gesturing to a cluster of shoots nearby.

Fletcher shook his head in amusement. "They're lilies. They grow all around here. Those over there, the taller ones, are daffodils. They've actually finished blooming, but they'll be back next year."

"Because they're perennials," Nora said, rather pleased with herself for knowing that.

"Right. Perennials come back on their own, annuals have to be replanted. Speaking of which, every year your grandmother gathered seeds from the annuals, especially the herbs. She said her mother did the same and so on back as far as anyone could remember. That means the same strains have been growing in this garden since Amelia first laid it out."

"That's unusual, isn't it?"

"Very. Most people just buy from the big seed manufacturers and let it go at that. You should try to find those seeds."

"There are some small cloth bags in the pantry. I'll bet that's what's in them."

Fletcher nodded. He stood up and dusted off his hands. "Let's find out."

It was dark and cool in the pantry. Nora flipped on the ceiling light, a single bare bulb. "This must be one of the oldest parts of the house," she said, glancing around at the roughly hewn wood walls hung with deep shelves.

"Seems like it," Fletcher agreed. "The herbs would have been dried in the attic and I'm sure there's a root cellar, but a lot of the family's food supply would have been stored here."

They found the cloth bags piled neatly on a shelf near the door. Inside each was a handwritten label.

"There are dozens here," Nora said. "Some of them I've never even heard of."

"That's the advantage of legacy seeds," Fletcher said. "You get a much broader variety."

"Is that what they're called—legacy seeds?"

He nodded. "There are people who collect them, trade them back and forth. I'll bet if you look through Liz's correspondence, you'll discover she was in touch with other gardeners like herself."

"I'll have to find out." She touched a finger gently to the tiny black seeds and thought of the life they would shortly bring. "When do I plant these?"

"You can start those now indoors, them move them out in a few weeks. Some of the others should wait a while yet."

He continued looking through the bags. "These are a real treasure. I wonder—" Abruptly he broke off.

"What?"

"Nothing. If we look around, I'm sure we'll find starter pots. Want to try?"

"Sure, but first I'd like to know what you were going to say."

He sighed. "I just wondered if the house goes back to the family and they turn it into a museum, whether they'll maintain the garden. Probably they will."

Nora went very still inside. It was the first time he had spoken of the future. But he had done so reluctantly, obviously unwilling to press her.

She let her breath out slowly. "I suppose so. Now where could those starter pots be?"

The seeds were planted and the garden looked far more alive when Fletcher left several hours later. It was, after all, Monday and they both had work to do.

"I've got to get some film to New York," he said, "but I'll be back this evening. How about dinner?"

"You're willing to trust my cooking again?"

"Actually, I thought I'd bring take-out."

She laughed and took a playful swat at him, but agreed. Once he was gone, the quiet of the house pressed in at her. It no longer seemed so peaceful, just empty and rather lonely.

Determined not to give in to such negative feelings, she got down to work. Charlotte might be talking about how rich she was going to be, but no one was paying her to sit around doing nothing. Besides, she couldn't stand that.

She was back in the Kincaid files, threading her way through the organizational maze, when she realized there was a gap in the information she had loaded on the hard drive. She'd tried to include everything she thought she might need before leaving the city, but there were several months worth of records for one particular sub-sub-subsidiary that she didn't have.

Fortunately she was more or less sure that they were on the mainframe back at the office. All she had to do was get them. "Thank heavens for modems," she murmured.

It should have been a simple task—call up the mainframe, tell it what she needed and download the appropriate files. But before she did that, she decided to make sure there was nothing else she'd overlooked. She began scanning the list of what she had.

Doing that meant checking what was on the hard drive and that was where the problem started. There were hundreds of files, but she'd worked with them enough that they were all at least somewhat familiar. All except one file buried in the middle of the list under an innocuous name: *Corres.*

Corres? Correspondence, she supposed. It was an ordinary enough name for a file except she couldn't remember it. She remembered *Letters* and the ever-popular *Misc,* dumping ground for everything that didn't have another place. But she couldn't recall ever having a file named *Corres.*

She especially didn't remember ever having secured such a file so that, when she tried to gain access to see what it contained, she was blocked.

The screen went blank, then flashed: *Password.*

It wasn't her file. That had to be the explanation. Somehow, she'd accidentally picked up someone else's data. She supposed the correct thing to do was delete it.

And she would have, except she couldn't. Not without the password. Of course, she could just ignore the whole thing, but curiosity was getting the better of her.

Nora smiled a little ruefully. Long ago—say two, three years—she had said goodbye to her hacker phase. Not that she'd ever gone in for any of the heavy stuff, but she'd taken a certain pleasure in coasting along the nooks and crannies of the information highway. Some of that skill hadn't left her.

It took more than an hour and a whole lot more effort than she'd expected when she started, but in the end the encryption program that locked *Corres* opened.

She was in. A flash of the old excitement made her sit up straighter, but she reminded herself she was just there to delete the file. Not that it would do any harm to find out first who it belonged to.

Except that she couldn't. *Corres* included no letters, no names, no hint of where it had come from. Corres was a program, a set of very sophisticated instructions to her little notebook, telling it to—

To what? A quick scan of the first hundred or so lines of code told her nothing. Nothing, that is, except that she needed to brush up on her programming. The explanation was in there. All she had to do was find it.

One pot of tea, two aspirins and a ham sandwich later, she had it. Nora flopped back in her chair, staring at the computer screen in astonishment. She'd been in some peculiar situations in her career, but this took the cake.

Her notebook was bugged. Someone—a very expert someone—had it primed to report exactly what she'd been doing. The moment she went on-line, to the mainframe, for instance, the little electronic monster was set to shoot out every detail of what files she'd been in, when and for how long.

Holy cow.

This was heavy stuff. The mole program—as she instantly thought of it—must have been somewhere in all the Kincaid files she'd loaded. It had to have been put in there precisely to track the audit.

She whistled softly. The implications kept coming. Logically the mole reported to her own firm's mainframe, the computer she could be expected to contact when she realized files were missing. They'd probably been deliberately omitted exactly to force her to go on-line.

But that meant that someone at Kincaid Industries had contact with her firm's information base, could reach into it and retrieve whatever her computer reported.

Nasty, very nasty.

No way was this the sort of thing someone would do out of idle curiosity. It was simply too complicated—not to mention illegal.

Okay, someone had to be sufficiently worried to want to know what she was doing.

Someone? The obvious person was Robert Kincaid, but he was unlikely to have the necessary technical ability. Not that he'd have any trouble finding someone to do it. For enough money, people would do anything.

Or he might know nothing about it. There could be someone else in his organization who was responsible.

Either way, she knew for certain what she'd already suspected—this wasn't an ordinary audit. This was going to be one of those she'd remember for a long time.

She backed out of the encryption program, leaving no trace so far as she could tell, and unplugged the phone line. No downloading for her. This time, she'd do it the old-fashioned way.

The secretary at work seemed a little surprised when Nora told her what she wanted. But it was only a few minutes work to copy some files to a diskette, stick it in a bag and send it off with a courier. Nora would get the information she needed, but she would leave nothing to trace her actions in the process.

That done, she sat back, rubbed her eyes and thought. Someone was going to wonder when she didn't connect to the mainframe. She had to hope whoever it was wouldn't get too impatient.

It was going to take time to get to the bottom of Kincaid Industries. But for sure it would be worth the effort.

Her fingers flew over the keys. Numbers danced in front of her. Smiling, she followed them.

Chapter 21

Nora moaned. She couldn't remember ever feeling this good. Well, actually she could, but not the same way.

"Down a little lower," she murmured. "Oh, that's it, that's great."

Fletcher's long, lean fingers massaged her back, rhythmically kneading out the tension. "Better?"

"Umph."

"I'll take that as a yes. What have you been doing to get yourself in knots like this?"

"Is that what I've done?"

"Sure have. I can feel them."

Nora sighed. She really was tired. The hours spent slogging her way through the Kincaid files had taken a toll. Worse yet, she couldn't honestly say she'd made much progress.

She should tell Fletcher that, explain that she needed to get back to work. There was so much to do and so little time.

But his touch was so distracting she wasn't having much luck forming a coherent thought. Besides, she could smell the Chinese food.

"What did you get?"

"Sesame chicken, Szechuan beef, pork in hot sauce and spring rolls."

"All for us?"

"I sure didn't invite anyone else. You?"

"Not me." His fingers hit a particularly sensitive spot. Her eyes closed blissfully.

"Food," he said and kissed her lightly on the cheek. She mustered enough coordination to stand and even managed to locate the plates.

They ate in front of the fireplace. It had gotten dark and a light rain was falling. Vivaldi played softly on the radio. "How was New York?" Nora asked.

"About as usual, loud, noisy and crowded."

"You really can't stand the place, can you?"

"Oh, I don't know. To tell you the truth, I took a walk up Fifth Avenue. It was actually enjoyable."

"What's this I'm hearing? Hamilton Fletcher says something nice about the big, bad city?"

"Hey, as long as I know I'm not stuck there, I can see its good points."

"Like what?" she asked, helping herself to another spring roll.

"There's a lot of energy and creativity, people working together to get things done."

"Any minute, the Chamber of Commerce is going to be on the phone."

"What about you? Are you missing the place?"

"I don't know," she admitted slowly. "The truth is, I haven't thought about it."

"You've been busy."

She met his eyes and blushed. He grinned and reached for the mustard.

Nora almost didn't say anything more. She really was tired and besides, it was so hard to concentrate when he was around. Still, she needed to talk to someone.

No, not just someone. She needed to talk to him, to share a part of herself, of who she was and what she did. She wanted him to understand.

Choosing her words with care, she said, "Actually I did have a busy day. This project is turning out to be more interesting than I'd expected."

"How so?"

"There's just more to it than the usual. I can't really say—"

"I understand," he interjected. "But if there's something you want to talk about—"

"What did you think of Robert Kincaid?"

"Great guy, salt of the earth."

"You're kidding?"

"Yeah, I am. He's a slick operator who's maybe gotten too used to winning."

"So that he thinks it's his right?"

"Possibly. He was coming on pretty hard to you at the party."

"Could be he's just real friendly."

"And this could be nursery school, but it isn't." He paused for a moment, then said, "Nora, I know you've been doing this kind of work for a while and you've probably encountered all sorts of things, but do both of us a favor and be a little more careful than you would be ordinarily."

"Why?"

"Just a feeling I have. Kincaid comes across as totally confident, successful, the guy who's got it made. But there's an edge under that. I can't put my finger on it, but it's almost as though he's trying too hard to project a certain image. If he really is the way he appears, why make such a big point of it?"

"Why isn't he more relaxed?"

"Exactly. Maybe it just isn't his temperament, but there could be something working at him."

"I thought you were good with animals. Seems like you understand people just as well."

"People are animals," he said. "We're motivated by the same drives—food, territory, a mate—plus a few extra. It's a good idea not to forget that."

"I'll try to remember," she said and realized she was staring at his mouth. He realized it, too, and smiled.

"Still hungry?"

"Yes," she said, and then pushed the food aside.

Shortly after Fletcher left the following morning, Nora took a look in the pantry and realized she needed to go shopping. It was just as well. Getting out for a while would do her good, maybe even blow away a few of the cobwebs cluttering her head.

Traffic was the usual mess along the main street, but she found a spot without too much trouble. Maybe she was getting better at this. In the market, she loaded up. The first time she shopped, she'd assumed she wouldn't be staying long. Now she assumed nothing. It was simpler that way.

With the groceries in the car, she started for home. Most people were at work. Once she was out of town, traffic was light. She got back a little more than an hour from when she'd left.

The first few bags were on the kitchen counter and she was returning to the car for more when she realized something was wrong. The computer had been moved. It was no longer in the same position on the table where she'd left it.

Or at least she didn't think it was. The difference was slight; her mind might be playing tricks. Slowly Nora walked over to the table and stared at the computer. It was slightly to the left of the chair, in an awkward place for anyone sitting there to work.

Maybe she'd bumped it at some point. Maybe Fletcher had. She put her hand on the closed lid. It was warm.

She hadn't used the computer since the previous evening. There was no way it could be warm.

Unless someone had come into the house and turned it on during her absence.

Disbelief shot through her. Following hard on it came fear. Abruptly it occurred to her that whoever had done it might not have left yet. She grabbed the computer and hurried out the door. Back in the car, she stared at the house and tried to decide what to do.

She had little to go on. A warm computer wasn't likely to impress the police. Besides, all things considered, she wasn't sure she wanted to involve them. The situation was delicate enough as it was. Yet neither was she going back in that house by herself. For the first time since she was a kid, she was facing a situation she didn't want to handle alone. Coincidentally—or not—she didn't have to.

Slowly she picked up the car phone and dialed Information. Fletcher's number was listed. He answered on the first ring.

"What's up?" he asked after she'd apologized for interrupting his work and he'd assured her it was no problem.

Nora hesitated. There was no sign of any movement in or around the house. She was beginning to feel a little foolish.

"I went shopping."

"That's good."

"When I came back, the computer I've been using was in a slightly different position on the table and it was warm."

He was silent for a moment. "When did you last use it?"

"Yesterday just before you came."

"Not anytime today?"

"Nope."

"Where are you?"

"In the car."

"Stay there, put up the windows and lock the doors. I'm on my way."

Three, maybe four minutes later, the Jeep pealed to a stop next to her. Fletcher got out. Without thought, Nora jumped from her car and went to him. His embrace was hard and fierce, but he put her aside quickly and looked toward the house.

"Anything?"

She shook her head. "The kitchen door was locked when I got home, I used my key."

"There are plenty of other ways to get in. Stay here." He started toward the house.

"Wait, I'm coming with you."

Fletcher didn't so much as glance at her. He simply said, "No, you're not. Go back to the car and stay there."

Nora stopped dead in her tracks. Relief at his presence warred with exasperation over his high-handed attitude. If he thought she was going to play the shrinking violet, dependent on the big, strong man to take care of her, he was wrong.

"What if there's more than one?" she asked as she came up behind him.

He scowled at her. "Then there'd be more reason for you to stay in the car."

"No."

A deep sigh escaped him. "How did I know this? All right, if you're coming along, at least keep your voice down."

Nora smiled. Point won, she was happy enough to be compliant. They went around to the front door. It was securely locked. So was the door leading down into the basement. The windows looked undisturbed. She was beginning to think her imagination really had been playing tricks on her when they came to the side door that led into the mudroom. Fletcher bent down and looked at it carefully.

"It's been jimmied," he said. "Look there."

Where he pointed, she could see tiny flecks of white wood where the paint had been chipped. The condition of the wood left no doubt that the damage was very recent.

Fletcher took a handkerchief from his pocket and wrapped it around the doorknob. "I don't really think whoever did this was dumb enough not to wear gloves, but you can't be too sure."

Gently he tried the door. It didn't budge. "It's been relocked," he said and put the handkerchief away. "You can relax. Whoever your visitor was, he's gone."

"Locking the door again on his way out?"

Fletcher nodded. "He covered his tracks." They went back around to the other side of the house and entered through the kitchen. Looking around, he asked, "Was anything else disturbed?"

"I don't know. As soon as I realized about the computer, I left."

"Let's take a look."

Nora nodded. She wanted to believe this was all just some sort of prank by local youngsters, but there was really very little hope of that. By the time they had searched the rest of the house, and determined that nothing was missing or out of place, she had to accept the truth.

"Whoever it was just wanted to break into the computer."

Fletcher nodded. "Sure looks that way. You're not hooked up to a modem?"

She knew what he was thinking. If she'd been connected to one, the break-in could have occurred electronically. There would have been no need to actually enter the house. But by deciding to stay off-line, she'd blocked that kind of access.

Nora took a deep breath. Quietly she said, "Yesterday, I found an encryption program buried in my files. It seemed intended to report my activities. As soon as I went on-line, it would download to the firm's mainframe. Anyone who knew how could pick it up from there."

Fletcher frowned. "Is it possible this is some way your firm has of keeping track of how much people are working when they're away from the office?"

"It could be," Nora said slowly. "But it's not likely. If I don't get the work done, it will be glaringly obvious. No one would have to go to that kind of trouble to spot it."

"Are you doing anything in addition to the Kincaid audit?"

"No."

They looked at each other. "I'll bring in the groceries," Fletcher said.

Nora nodded. It was going to be a long night.

Chapter 22

Nora blinked once, twice, then again. Her eyes burned and her vision was blurred. She had been staring at the computer screen for so many hours that she was no longer sure what she was seeing.

It was deep into the night. Fletcher had made coffee and sandwiches but neither had wanted much. He'd searched the house again, just to be sure, then informed her he was staying.

She didn't argue. Just having him close by made her feel safer and even to a certain degree saner, as though work in all its craziness was no longer her entire life.

He built a fire in the parlor. She moved the notebook in there and camped out on a small table. The light of the computer screen was pale and ghostly compared to the glowing embers of the fire.

Fletcher was asleep. He'd stretched out on the couch and dozed off an hour or so ago. When she realized he'd fallen asleep, she spread an afghan over him, touched his hair lightly and went back to work.

Whoever had broken into her computer was damn good, but they hadn't counted on her own instincts. Working in the business she did, with the responsibilities she carried, she had long ago installed a way to track which files were used and when. The intruder had found it, of course, and tried to circumvent it.

But she'd been just creative enough to fool him. He undoubtedly thought he'd deleted all evidence of his presence, but he was wrong. She could still follow a shadowy trail that led straight through her own records, showing where she'd been, everything she'd looked at, gone back to, puzzled over.

Thank God she hadn't made any notes. She carried it all in her head, all her suspicions about Kincaid Industries, the unnatural complexity of the organization and the places she suspected were the most questionable.

She'd left nothing written down, but to anyone clever enough to decipher them, her own movements could make her thinking clear. Anyone who really knew what was going on at Kincaid Industries would be able to judge how close she was getting to finding that out for herself.

The anyone had to be Robert Kincaid or someone acting on his behalf. It had to be. Nothing else made any sense. The trouble was she had to be able to prove it. Before she blew the whistle, she had to have evidence to back her up.

Nora ran a hand through her short auburn hair and tried to focus better. The answer had to lie in the mole program. If she could figure out who it was supposed to report to, she'd have what she needed.

Fletcher moved slightly on the couch. Distracted, she gazed at him. Tired as she was, almost numb really, he enthralled her. His sheer physical size and strength was so at odds with his innate gentleness and the intelligence of his nature. He seemed almost impossibly perfect, far too good to be true.

Too good for her?

She sat up a little straighter, as though prodded. Where had that particularly nasty thought come from? She'd never had a problem judging her own self-worth. Had she?

But neither had she ever ventured much from her own little niche, preferring to stay where she felt capable and in control. Until now.

Standing up, she went over to prod the fire. Exhaustion made her feel light-headed. If she tried to drink more coffee, she'd drown. She settled for cold water splashed on her face at the kitchen sink.

When she returned to the parlor, she did seem a little more alert. At least enough so that after a few minutes of staring at the mole program, she thought she saw something she hadn't before.

She'd presumed that whoever was responsible for tracking her movements would have to retrieve that information from her firm's mainframe. That much was true, but now she saw that the program was fixed to call in automatically and download the information it had gleaned.

Call where?

It took her four tries and some of the fanciest footwork she'd ever attempted inside the whirligig world of a computer, but in the end she had what she was looking for.

Well, no, she didn't because when the decoded phone number finally popped up on the screen, Nora stared at it in disbelief. She recognized it immediately. It was the same number she'd gotten from information the previous day.

Fletcher's number.

Dawn again. Nora sat with her knees drawn up to her chin, staring out at the water. She had come down to the beach to think. It wasn't going too well.

Of course, it didn't help that she was so tired she felt as though she was stumbling through a surreal scene where everything was just slightly out of kilter. Her chest hurt. She felt as though she'd been crying for a long time, so much so that her ribs ached and her insides seemed bruised.

But she hadn't shed a tear and she didn't intend to. The last time she'd done that she was eleven years old and had ridden her bike headlong into a tree.

That she was experiencing a somewhat similar sensation right then didn't matter. She wasn't going to cry.

She was going to face up to the situation and decide what to do about it.

Fletcher could be working for Robert Kincaid.

That was the hard, ugly possibility that made her stomach heave.

The way he'd come into he life had been so convenient, banishing her natural caution and leading her to trust him implicitly. It horrified her to think how gullible she might have been.

Even that little scene at the party when Fletcher had appeared annoyed by Kincaid's interest in her could have been arranged. Every step of the way she could have been lulled into a sense of false security, dazed by sensual satisfaction and the gentler but equally potent sense of no longer being alone.

It could have happened like that.

But that didn't mean it had.

She'd have to be crazy to take anything at face value. All her instincts—the same ones she'd relied on since she was a kid—told her that Hamilton Fletcher was a good, decent man. She could be wrong, but she wasn't about to jump to conclusions.

She needed a plan, a way to find out conclusively what was going on. Wearily she put her head in her hands. All around her, the world was coming back to life. Birds pranced at the water's edge and soared above, the wind stirred branches heavy with buds. From the copse of oaks, a deer peered at her.

She watched it from between her fingers until it withdrew into the forest. When it was gone, she stood and looked toward the house. Nothing of it was visible except the twin brick chimneys rising over the treetops.

Had Amelia Daniels looked upon the same scene? The house had been added onto several times, but the two chimneys were both very old, and there had been plenty of time for trees to grow, die and be replaced.

There was a good chance that the women of her family down through all the generations had stood where she stood and seen what she saw.

As tired as she was in the first bright light of day she no longer felt entirely alone. There seemed to be a presence all around her, part of the sun and sea, and the land itself. The presence of wise, strong women who had not feared to love—or live.

The fatigue that had weighed her down seemed to slip away. She stood, straightened her shoulders and walked back toward the house.

Fletcher was making coffee. His hair was rumpled, his shirt pulled out and he needed a shave. He looked glorious.

"Any luck?" he asked when he saw her.

"Depends." She took the coffee can from him and finished the job. When the pot was on, she said, "I want to show you something."

They went back to the parlor. "Sit down," she said, pointing to the chair in front of the small table she'd been using.

He did so, looking puzzled.

"I noticed a computer on your worktable. Do you program?"

"Some." He sounded cautious, not sure where she was going. That scared her some, but she ignored it and went on.

"Remember the encryption program I found?"

"Of course."

"It was set to download information."

"Where to?"

"Your computer."

Under other circumstances, the look on his face would have been comical. "You're kidding?"

"Nope. It was encrypted along with everything else, but that's your number, all right."

"That's crazy."

The absolute flat certainty with which he said that reassured her. She rested a hand on his shoulder and looked at the screen. "The way I figure it, my visitor yesterday may not have just come to collect information. He left a little of his own."

"May not have?"

"Sorry, force of habit. He switched whatever the real number was and put yours in instead."

Until that moment, she hadn't really felt the tension in him. But now it evaporated. His shoulders actually dropped in relief. Taking her hand in his, he stood.

His eyes really were the most remarkable shade of blue, especially when he smiled. "Thank you," he said simply.

Her throat tightened. She looked away long enough to make sure she wasn't going to make a total fool of herself. Candidly she said, "It took me a while to figure out."

"How long a while?"

"A few hours."

"That's not bad. After all, we haven't known each other very long."

"You're being generous. I should have realized right away."

His smile deepened. "Okay, you should have. But I'll give you this one."

"Wait a second, I was thinking I could try to find some way to make it up to you."

"That wouldn't involve cooking, would it?"

She slipped her hands up under his shirt, stroking the warm, smooth skin. "Why, are you hungry?"

"Starving," he said, and drew her hard against him.

Chapter 23

Fletcher's hand cupped her bottom. He lifted her leg, his own sliding between her thighs. "You know what I really like first thing in the morning?"

"Coffee?"

"Better than that."

The friction of his jeans rubbing against her sent heat stabbing upward. Her fingers clenched in his shirt as she fought the urge to remove it with unladylike haste. Beneath her back, the plaster of the wall was cool and smooth.

Dust motes danced in the sunlight coming in through the windows at either end of the second-floor hallway. They'd gotten that far with most of their clothes still on, but that wasn't going to last much longer.

His tongue teased the sensitive skin at the base of her neck before drifting lower, laving her nipples to hardness. She gasped and grazed his shoulder lightly with her teeth.

"A nice, warm shower," he said. "That's what we both need."

She licked the tiny cut still visible on his chin. "Absolutely, but we wouldn't want to waste water."

His hands grasped her waist, lifting her slightly up and then down against him. "Wouldn't be ecologically sound."

"Environmentally responsible."

"Whatever." He raised her quickly in his arms and carried her down the hall toward the bathroom. Kicking open the door, he stopped, still holding her, and looked around in renewed bemusement.

The bath was a holdover from the previous century. Easily as big as a fair-sized bedroom, it included its own marble-manteled fireplace, a plush Oriental rug and a genuine, cast-iron Victorian-style tub complete with claw feet.

Wooden cabinets discreetly concealed a commode and sink. Large potted plants were clustered near the windows. There was even an elaborately carved Chinese chest beside the tub containing a variety of lotions, oils and soaps.

A shower attachment hung above the tub. Fletcher set her down gently and without letting go of her, flicked the water on. He pulled the curtain closed. Almost at once, steam began billowing into the room.

"You must be exhausted," he said, undoing her shirt. "Let me help you."

In fact, she was astonishingly wide-awake, all things considered. But far be it from her to turn down a helping hand—or two. Especially when they were so delightfully occupied.

"Thanks so much," she murmured as he removed the shirt. Beneath it she wore a delicate, pink silk bra trimmed with tiny rosebuds. Fletcher grinned when he saw it. He undid the front clasp. Her breasts slipped into his hands. He teased the nipples gently, watching as they hardened even further.

"Beautiful," he murmured. His voice was thick. The light in his eyes had turned hard and bright.

Quickly he stripped away her slacks. His jeans followed. When they were both naked, he lifted her and stepped under the shower. The water was hot enough to sting slightly. Nora gasped as it poured over them both. She tilted her head back, closing her eyes.

And opened them to the smell of roses as full and heady as a summer day. Fletcher poured oil from a small bottle. He moistened his palms, then rubbed them lightly over her throat and breasts. The sensation was exquisite. She felt as though she was melting from the inside out.

Slowly, with infinite care, Fletcher massaged the scented oil all over her. Not an inch of her body was neglected. Long before he was done, Nora was trembling. She doubted her legs could hold her much longer. When his hand slipped between them to stroke the oil into the nest of curls there, she cried out.

"No more, please. I can't stand this."

"Neither can I," he said and reached to turn the water off. Lifting her from the tub, he took a large, fluffy bath sheet and began to dry her. The slightly abrasive touch of the cloth against her fully aroused body was too much for Nora. She grabbed hold of his hands to stop him and pressed her body against his.

They moved together, wet and hot, skin slick from the water and the oil. The scent of roses was everywhere. He laid her on the rug and slipped between her legs. At the first touch of him, pleasure uncoiled throughout her. She took him in her hand, urging him, and cried out softly.

Braced on his arms above her, he moved slowly, each thrust controlled, measured. Again and again, he entered her, stroking her pleasure to unparalleled heights. There were roses everywhere, roses and summer, heat and bright, pearl white light exploding within her.

From a great distance, Nora heard herself cry out. She fell away into soft, welcoming darkness.

When she awoke, her first thought was astonishment, as though she had been completely unaware of sleeping. Sitting up, she glanced around quickly.

She was in the bedroom, alone in the big bed. Beneath the silken sheet and downy blanket, she was naked. The bedspread had been neatly folded back. The curtains were drawn across the windows.

Nora moved slowly. Her body felt almost overwhelmingly fragile. Drawing the blanket with her, she got out of bed and walked over to a window. Beyond the billowing curtain, a sun-bright day beckoned. She glanced at the clock on the dressing table. It was mid-afternoon.

With a gasp, she hurried over to the closet and pulled out the first clothes she touched. Dressed in old jeans and a comfortable sweater, she went downstairs.

There was no sign of Fletcher. A note on the kitchen table said: Gone to look after the houseguests. Back soon. Keep the doors locked. F.

Houseguests. That would be the opossum and the falcon. She sighed and let the note drop. There was no way of knowing when he'd left or how much longer he'd be gone. She was on her own, at least for the moment.

That should be fine. She was certainly used to it and she needed some time to get over the strange, lingering sense of vulnerability with which she'd awakened. Fletcher had left coffee in a thermos. Silently giving thanks for his thoughtfulness, she poured a cup and drank it standing at the kitchen window.

She should fix something to eat, make a few phone calls, get back to work. There was laundry to do, it wouldn't hurt to dust, the garden still needed weeding. There was more than enough to keep her occupied.

The problem was she couldn't seem to bestir herself to do anything. She didn't feel tired so much as lethargic, as though all the energy and drive had been burned out of her.

A slight smile curved her mouth. There wasn't any big mystery about how that had happened. If Gramma Liz had known what her Victorian bathroom would provoke, she might have been tempted to renovate.

No, on second thought, she probably would have cheered.

Gramma Liz had liked Fletcher. Nora had no doubts about that. She would have approved of him. Smiling more broadly, Nora raised her coffee cup in a toast to the interesting—and inspirational—legacy the women of her family had left.

Charlotte and others like her might be out to make them all seem like cardboard cutouts, but they'd been women who lived with passion. And they'd shown a definite fondness for men like Fletcher.

When she came right down to it, she was just being true to her heritage. With a soft laugh, she popped two pieces of bread into the toaster and refilled her coffee cup. Anything more substantial could wait.

Nora was spreading jam on the toast when the phone rang. It was Robert Kincaid—again.

"Hi, there," he said, sounding relaxed and good-humored. "What are you up to?"

She stiffened. He was absolutely the last person she wanted to talk to, but he was also an important client of the firm. She couldn't simply hang up on him. Cautiously she said, "Hi, I'm just having lunch."

She had the vague hope that he might apologize for interrupting such an obviously important activity and cut the call short. But either lunch wasn't one of Kincaid's priorities or he wasn't big on hints. Instead he said, "I'm glad I caught you in. I was talking with Dave Marsdon this morning."

Dave Marsdon was one of the top partners of Nora's firm. He was known to make and break the careers of younger staff members at will.

As casually as she could manage, she said, "Oh, really?"

"That's right. He seemed a little surprised to hear you were up here."

Nora bit back a groan. Marsdon was rigidly conventional. In his mind, you weren't working unless you were parked behind a desk where the senior partners could keep an eye on you and make sure they were getting their dollar's worth. The notion that someone could do a thoroughly competent job in their own home, working their own hours, struck him as nothing more than bizarre.

"I don't actually report to him," she said, "so he wouldn't necessarily be aware of my assignment."

"He's aware of it now. I told him I was sure you were doing a great job."

"Thanks, I appreciate that." The same way she appreciated a really bad headache.

"You know, it occurred to me, Marsdon's a great guy, plays a hell of a squash game, but he's not necessarily cut out to appreciate intelligence and initiative. You know what I mean?"

"I'm not sure—"

"Just that big accounting firms aren't exactly known for being on the cutting edge, are they? Fact is, they can be downright stodgy. A bright woman like yourself might do a whole lot better elsewhere."

He was good, Nora thought. She had to give him that. The fact was she wasn't convinced she wanted to stay with the firm long-term. The chances of someone like herself making partner were dim and besides, that wasn't all it was cracked up to be. She had the feeling she might be better off in a less conservative organization or maybe even a business of her own.

But she hadn't told that to anyone, least of all to Robert Kincaid. All the same, he seemed to have picked up on some measure of her discontent and was willing to exploit it.

"I'm pretty comfortable where I am," she hedged.

He laughed. "You don't strike me as the sort who's interested in comfort. You like a challenge, don't you? Well, I've got plenty of them. Kincaid Industries is always looking for someone with your abilities."

"I see—"

"Why don't we get together and talk about it? Say, dinner tonight?"

He phrased that as a question, but the gesture was hollow. Obviously he expected her to jump at the chance for such a discussion.

Nora did anything but. She was immensely suspicious of his motives, but even if she hadn't been, she already knew enough about Kincaid Industries to know she didn't want to work there.

"I appreciate the suggestion," she said. "But—"

"But what?" Kincaid interrupted. His tone was harder, with a dawning note of disbelief. "You're not going to tell me you have other plans again."

"I'm afraid I do. I have to work."

"That's absurd. You were too busy two days ago and now you're telling me you can't get away this evening? What is this?"

Nora took a deep breath. The time had come to talk more frankly with Mr. Robert Kincaid, but she needed to do it carefully. "I'm not happy with the idea of our seeing each other for any purpose while I'm doing the audit on your company. It raises the potential of conflict of interest.''

His laugh was hard and cold. "Let me get this straight, you're turning me down—*me*—because of some *ethical* concern?''

"Yes, I am. I hope you understand.''

"I don't believe this. Don't you realize this is the chance of a lifetime for you? You're going to throw it away because of some pissant code of conduct no one in their right mind would give a thought to?''

"I give it a thought," Nora said softly, "and so do a whole lot of other people I know. If you and I have anything to talk about, we should be able to do it just as well after I complete the audit.''

"Listen,'' Kincaid snarled. "I do things on my timetable, not anybody else's. When I ask a woman out, she comes. And when I tell someone they can have a job with me, they jump. You got that?''

Oh, yeah, she had it perfectly. He was an insufferable boor, a man so full of himself that he couldn't see anything beyond his own desires. Or fears.

"You've made yourself very clear, Mr. Kincaid,'' Nora said quietly. "Now if you'll excuse me, I have to get back to work.''

He made a sound of disgust. "You do that, Ms. Delaney.'' The phone slammed down.

Nora hung up slowly. Her stomach was clenched and she felt queasy. Going head-to-head with an egocentric millionaire who had enormous clout all through the business world was not her favorite thing to do, especially when that same man might be involved in illegal enterprises he did not want her to discover.

She could have been more conciliatory, tried to lull him into a false sense of security. But she was no good at that kind of thing. All her life she'd dealt with issues directly and never had cause to regret it. But then she'd also dealt with people who were more or less sane.

There was something about Kincaid, something in the way he had flown off the handle as soon as he realized she wasn't falling in with his wishes, that made her realize he could be dangerous.

He hadn't built an empire in just a few short years by being a nice guy. There were signs throughout the information she'd been studying of ruthless acquisitions, a pattern of getting what he wanted at any cost.

If he felt all that was now threatened, what might he do?

With a sigh, she wrapped her arms around herself and wondered when Fletcher would be back.

Chapter 24

Fletcher murmured in his sleep, turned over and drew Nora closer. Snuggled against him, his arm around her waist, she relaxed a little. But not much. Despite having slept so late into the day, she should have been tired. All the work and worry—not to mention the ways she and Fletcher found to entertain each other—had taxed her strength. But sleep remained elusive.

She lay, eyes open, staring at the curtains moving gently on the night wind. It bothered her that she hadn't told Fletcher about Kincaid's call. But she'd been so glad to see him and she'd wanted to know all about how the opossum was doing and the falcon, too, of course, and he'd been hungry and made dinner and afterward... Well, afterward she'd forgotten.

Now she remembered. He'd be upset when he found out she hadn't told him. He'd expect her to confide in him. It was all part of being together in—heaven help her—a relationship.

She was no good at this sort of thing. She had no real experience at it. There were no manuals, no tutorials that she knew of. She couldn't boot up the computer and find answers to the ticklish questions of the human heart.

She shifted slightly, wiggling into a more comfortable position. Doing so brought her bottom into even closer contact with Fletcher. Did he ever wear pajamas? Probably not; he seemed naturally warm-blooded. She smiled at the thought.

Her eyelids were growing heavier. Perhaps she could sleep after all. She was just sliding away into dreams when a faint, elusive impression jarred her.

Something was wrong.

Slowly, careful not to disturb Fletcher, she sat up. Her imagination must be playing tricks on her. The house was quiet, wrapped in night. She lay back down, but a moment later, she was up again. Her whole body stiffened.

She smelled smoke.

Not the same kind as when she'd left the flue closed, but something harsher, more acrid, with an almost greasy feel to it. It was smoke all the same. And where there was smoke, there was—

"Oh, my God!"

Nora jumped from the bed and grabbed for her clothes. Pulling them on with one hand, she shook Fletcher with the other. "Fletcher, get up! There's a fire!"

He woke instantly, no grogginess and no questions. One look at her was enough. He was out of the bedroom door, pants in his hand. Nora followed at a run.

"Downstairs," he said. She nodded. The smell was more distinct now. It led them to the fire.

It was outside, up against one side of the house where a small addition had been built years ago. Part of one wall was already burning and it was spreading fast.

"Liz kept fire extinguishers in the kitchen," Fletcher said. He had to raise his voice above the roar of the fire.

As Nora raced to get them, he was yanking bushes and other ground cover away from the wall, denying the fire that much fuel.

She was back in moments, having found three extinguishers. She tossed one to Fletcher and took another for herself. Silently praying that Liz hadn't let them expire, she tore off the clip, aimed the nozzle and fired.

Instantly a stream of fire-smothering chemicals shot out. Where it hit, the flames died. Fletcher finished one and grabbed another. "It's not enough," he said. "Get buckets. We'll need to wet down the whole wall." As she ran to obey, he shouted, "And blankets!"

Desperation filled her. Frantically she grabbed blankets out of the upstairs linen closet and ripped them off the beds. Tossing them out of the window to Fletcher, she ran back outside. Racing through the kitchen, she took a few precious moments to call 911.

Outside Fletcher was using a blanket to beat back the fire where it tried to spring up again. Nora found the outside faucet and began filling buckets. She ran back and forth, handing them to him, for what seemed like forever but was probably only a few minutes.

Off in the distance, sirens sounded.

An hour later the fire was out and quiet was returning to the house. Nora and Fletcher stood at the side of the house and surveyed the damage.

Most of one wall on the addition was charred or entirely gone. But the flames had been contained to it. They hadn't reached the roof or spread beyond.

"We were lucky," Nora said softly.

Fletcher nodded. He put an arm around her waist and drew her closer. He smelled of smoke and was covered with grime. It streaked his face, arms and bare chest.

Nora knew she looked much the same. They were exhausted and filthy, but they'd saved the house. Alone, she could never have done it.

Softly, against his chest, she murmured, "Thank you."

He looked down at her, puzzled. "For what?"

"For what you did, of course. I'd never have been able to put it out by myself." She touched his face lightly, tracing the curve of his jaw. The roughness felt tantalizing beneath her fingers. "I'm so glad you're here."

He made a hard sound and pulled her back into his arms. They stood like that, staring at the damaged wall, for several moments.

"You know this wasn't an accident," Fletcher said finally.

Nora nodded. "The firemen made that clear." An inspector had already examined the remains, taking samples of the wall and the ground in front of it. There would be tests done, but no one had any doubts that it was arson. As the inspector had said, an accelerant had been splashed on the wall and lit. If the wood had been drier, if their response had been slower, the entire house could have gone up.

"Charlotte's going to have a fit when she hears about this."

Fletcher laughed. "Her worst fears confirmed?"

"Something like that, but it's not funny. I've only been here a few days and the house could have been destroyed twice."

"You're not counting that thing with the fireplace?"

"Of course I am. How do you think I'd feel if I turned out to be the one person who inherited Amelia's house and couldn't protect it properly?"

His arm tightened around her gently. "You're being way too hard on yourself. Far from being a danger to this house, you may be the only person who can really keep it from harm."

"There's not a lot of evidence for that right now."

"Sure there is. What about the danger of this place being turned into a museum?"

"That's not in quite the same league as it being burned down."

"True enough, but it still wasn't your fault."

"Yes," she said quietly, "it was. You know as well as I do who probably did this, or paid for it at least."

They were on slippery ground now and both realized it. She was about to accuse an extremely powerful man of an extremely serious crime. It was one thing to suspect it herself, but it was entirely another to confide that information to anyone else.

"Let's go inside," she said.

The kitchen was dark and smelled of wet smoke. Fletcher opened several windows to air it out while Nora made coffee. It was getting on for dawn. Everything seemed to happen then, she thought as she spooned grounds into the filter. She used to have such a nice, sane, predictable life. Nothing much ever really disrupted it. Now everything was different.

Absolutely everything.

Fletcher sat down at the table. He had washed the worst of the grime from his face, but his chest was still streaked with it. Some of the golden hair was singed and there were several angry, red streaks where embers had fallen on him.

Nora's mouth went dry. Instinctively she reached out to touch him. "I didn't realize—"

"It's nothing."

Maybe not, but she hurt inside at the thought of him being endangered. Damn Robert Kincaid and the whole stupid mess. She was going to put an end to it once and for all.

Something smelled at Kincaid Industries. Hell, it stank. She was going to find out what it was and blow the lid sky-high. She'd put that bastard in jail for the rest of his life. He deserved that much for putting Fletcher at risk, never mind anything else he'd done.

There was just one problem.

"When are you going to tell the police?" Fletcher asked.

Nora hesitated. He wasn't going to like her answer but he was going to have to accept it anyway.

"I suspect Robert Kincaid of being responsible for the break-in of this house and my computer, and I believe that when that didn't secure the information he wanted, he decided to either try to scare me into keeping my mouth shut or worse."

Fletcher's eyes hardened. "Worse being your death."

"And yours. But whether that's what he intended or not, the fact remains that all I've got are suspicions. I don't have any evidence."

"You've got the mole program."

"With your phone number on it."

He sighed. "What about Kincaid Industries itself? Obviously he's got something to hide."

"I agree, but I still don't know exactly what it is."

"How close are you?"

"I don't know."

He looked grim. "I don't like this. The hell with evidence. Kincaid could have killed you."

"So what do you suggest? The authorities wouldn't even listen to me at this point."

He didn't reply—exactly. But the way he looked at her was a shock. It made her realize how very thin the veneer of civilization could be with him. In another age, men like Fletcher wouldn't have hesitated to handle such a situation by themselves. He was capable of enormous tenderness—she knew that full well.

But there was also a ruthlessness about him that could be deadly.

"Don't," she said.

He raised his eyebrows. "Don't what?"

"Try to handle this by yourself."

His mouth quirked. He looked amused. *"Try?"*

At that moment, she realized how little she really knew about this man. There were whole aspects of his life that remained closed to her. She had a sudden, flashing image of him alone in the wilderness, pitted against the might of nature, and enjoying it. Compared to all that, Robert Kincaid might not seem like much of a challenge.

"There's a possibility I'm wrong," she said, almost desperately.

"I don't think so."

His confidence warmed her even as she feared where it might lead.

"Look," she said, "what if I tell my firm that the audit's complete and I'm just staying on here a few days to wrap up loose ends on the house? I can give the impression that Kincaid Industries passed with flying colors."

"What good will that do?"

"My guess is it will take about five minutes to get back to Kincaid. He'll figure I got the message."

Fletcher looked unconvinced. "It's dangerous."

"So's life." She was just beginning to really appreciate that. Life without risks wasn't life at all; it was just existence. She'd played it safe for too long.

"I can do this," she said. "Kincaid Industries is ready to pop, I can feel it. A few days would probably do it."

Fletcher hesitated. She could see the war he was waging within himself and she held her breath. To agree, he needed to trust her.

"All right," he said slowly. "A few days. But after that, Kincaid will get suspicious again. Is there anything I can do to help?"

"I hate to say it—"

"What?"

Nora forced a lightness to her voice that she was far from feeling. She even managed to smile. "I hate to say it, Hamilton Fletcher, but you are the worst distraction I've ever encountered. Nothing else has even come close. When you're around, I have trouble remembering to breathe, much less keeping my mind on work."

He looked at her in astonishment. Abruptly he threw back his leonine head and laughed.

"I'm glad you're amused, but I'm serious. I have a lot of work to do and very little time to get it done. If you're around, forget it. I might as well throw in the towel now."

"I'm not sure whether I should be flattered or angry."

"Flattered, definitely. But do it somewhere else. You can't imagine what it's costing me to say this, but I need some time alone."

He stood up slowly, a grimy, smoke-streaked marvel of a man with eyes torn from the sky and a spirit that made her believe all things were possible.

Quietly he said, "All right, Nora Delaney, you've got what you want. But three days, no longer."

It was on the tip of her tongue to tell him she'd reconsidered. She was crazy to even consider such a thing. But she forced herself to stay silent. There was no other way.

Watching him walk out the door a few minutes later was the hardest thing she'd ever done. The hard, demanding kiss he bestowed on her right before leaving didn't make it any easier.

Chapter 25

"That's right," Nora said into the phone. "A few more days. Call it personal time. I have to wrap up these loose ends on the house."

Her manager at the firm—a young, aggressive partner named Bill Hobart—grunted. "That should be okay. You're sure the Kincaid audit's wrapped?"

"Good as," Nora hedged. She needed to be able to say afterward that something had been bothering her, a niggling sense that all was not quite right. It might not work, but she had to leave the door open.

"No problems?" Hobart pushed. He'd made partner the previous year and was eager to show he deserved it.

Nora forced a soft laugh. "What's the matter, Bill? You disappointed?"

"God, no. I just want to be sure, that's all. If you say it's done and clean, that's fine. So how much time do you think you need?"

"Like I said, a few days. With my grandmother dying and all—"

"Right, of course." Reassured about the audit, Hobart switched to his understanding mode. "Take whatever time you need. Stuff's piling up here a bit, but I trust your judgment."

Translation: Be back within a week or there'll be a problem.

Nora sighed. She'd squeaked past, but with no breathing room. There was no time to waste.

She made sure to thank Hobart all the same. By the time she hung up, she could tell he believed everything was fine. She didn't doubt that he'd report the Kincaid job as finished.

Message sent, she got down to work. Somewhere in the mounds of information she had available there was a key, a clue to show her which way to go. She had to find it fast.

But before she could get very far, the sound of a car pulling up outside stopped her. Impatiently, she jumped up and went to see who it was.

Patrick Delaney was getting out of an ancient convertible that looked to have had much love—and even more money—lavished on it. With a sigh, Nora went to open the door. She liked the man instinctively, but he'd picked a bad time to drop by.

He seemed to sense that the moment he glimpsed her forced smile. "Sorry to bother you," he said, "but I just came out to be sure you're all right."

Nora relaxed a little. The demands of work didn't override her appreciation for his thoughtfulness.

"I take it you heard what happened?" she asked.

Patrick laughed softly. "Me and everyone else. Don't worry, I headed Charlotte off."

"She was coming?"

"Bet on it. But I told her she'd already stuck her oar in more than enough."

Nora smiled. "I'm surprised that was enough to stop her."

"Maybe I put it a little more firmly than that. Anyway, how're you doing?"

"Okay. It was pretty frightening, though." Looking at him frankly, she said, "I'm glad Fletcher was here."

Patrick nodded. "He's a good man. Any idea how it happened?"

"The fire inspector thinks it was arson."

Patrick paled. He shook his head slowly. "We've never had anything like that around here."

A twinge of guilt went through Nora. Of course they hadn't. She'd brought it with her. "I'm sure the authorities will get to the bottom of it. In the meantime, we're taking precautions."

He didn't ask what they were, apparently accepting that she'd have the situation in hand. Neither did he ask who "we" might be. That was obvious.

"Where's Fletcher?"

Nora hesitated. She couldn't tell Patrick the truth, it was just too complicated. "He had to get some work done," she said finally. "He'll be back. Why don't I show you what happened?"

They went around to the side of the house where the fire had occurred. When Patrick saw the charred wall, he whistled softly. "Looks like it went just short of the roof."

Nora nodded. "At least it was a newer part of the house. The fire inspector thought we'd be able to fix the damage without any problem."

"Don't see why not. It doesn't even look as though the whole wall has to be replaced." He chuckled. "I hate to be the one to break it to Charlotte, but this old house has been through a hell of a lot more."

"Really?"

"Why sure. At least a couple of real bad hurricanes that I know of including the one that cut the channel through. Then there were several fires, mostly just from carelessness. When people had open fires in their houses all the time, that kind of thing was bound to happen."

He touched a hand to the side of the house affectionately. "No, this place has stood it all. It's been through revolution and civil war, not to mention maybe a couple of hundred kids growing up in it. If they weren't enough to wreck a house, a little bitty fire sure won't do it."

Nora laughed. "I never thought of that."

Patrick looked at her thoughtfully. "Well, maybe you ought to. Anyway, I've got to run. I'll tell Charlotte there's nothing for her to come sticking her nose into."

"I'd appreciate that," Nora said dryly. She walked back with him to the front yard. When he had gone, the old convertible tooling down the road, it seemed

very quiet. The sky was clear and a gentle breeze blew.
It was a day to be out in the garden, pulling up weeds
and deciding where to plant.

Instead she went back into the kitchen and forced
herself to get back to work. This was what she'd always loved doing, but now it seemed stale and dry. If
there hadn't been so much at stake, she would have
said it was even boring.

There was a frustration growing in her, a desire to
reach out to a broader life, that she couldn't think
about just then. In the silence, she could hear the
grandfather clock ticking on the stair landing. It was
an unnecessary reminder of time passing.

Hours passed. Nora barely moved. She got up to get
some lemonade and go to the bathroom, and that was
it. The world narrowed down to the computer screen
and the steady stream of information pouring out of
it. Slowly but surely, she was going back, following her
own footsteps through the maze of Kincaid Industries, seeing where she had first become suspicious,
first caught the scent of wrongdoing.

There, on the checks drawn just below the reporting limits. That's when she'd started to wonder. She
went deeper, tracing the sub-sub-subsidiaries, watching the flow of money back and forth, watching where
it disappeared.

Right there.

Abruptly she sat up straighter and stared at the
screen. She was looking at an apparently small and
obscure company that was based offshore on one of
the Caribbean islands. For an outfit that seemed to do

nothing, it sure took in a tremendous amount of money.

Money that seemed to just vanish. There were absolutely no records to indicate where it went. Dead end.

She sat back, thinking hard. This could be it or it could be nothing. There might be records, perfectly legal explanations for what she saw. She just might not have them.

In downloading so many files to her computer, it was possible she'd overlooked some. They could still be in the firm's mainframe. All she had to do was look.

If Kincaid believed the audit was done and he was safe, there shouldn't be any problem. No one should notice her make a quick dash in and out to see what she might have overlooked.

If.

Slowly she picked up the phone and punched in Bill Hobart's number. It was well after five, but he answered on the first ring. There might have been a senior partner calling.

He sounded disappointed when he realized who it was but recovered quickly. "Everything okay?" he asked. Hobart always sounded faintly worried. It went with being let just in the partnership door, far enough to glimpse all the goodies that lay beyond but not quite close enough to touch very many of them.

"Fine," she said quickly. "I'm sorry to bother you." She thought fast. What possible reason could she have for calling? "I just wanted to let you know

I'm making progress on the house. I probably won't need as many days as I thought."

"Great, that's great. I always said you were top-notch. In fact, I was just telling Dave Marsdon that this morning. He was real pleased that the Kincaid audit's been wrapped up."

"So you told him?"

"That's right. He and Kincaid play squash together. In fact, they had a game this afternoon. I figured it wouldn't hurt to pass the word."

Nora let her breath out slowly. Marsdon was a stickler, no hint of wrongdoing had ever been attached to his name. That was, at least, in part why he'd been put in charge of the audit side of the firm after the savings and loan stink. But that notwithstanding, it would have been perfectly reasonable to him to mention in passing that the audit was completed.

Kincaid knew. He had to think he'd won.

"That's fine," she said. "I won't keep you."

She hung up a moment later, unplugged the phone and connected the line to the computer. A few keystrokes later, she was into the mainframe.

Her search was quick and fruitful. Within minutes, she found the pieces she'd been missing. Not too long after that, she watched as they fell into place almost by themselves. The pattern of Robert Kincaid's deception became clear.

She had him.

Chapter 26

Nora hesitated, trying to decide what to do. It was really too late to call anyone. Besides, this really wasn't the sort of thing she could do over the phone. It had to be handled in person.

But first, she desperately needed to sleep. Carefully she recorded exactly what she'd done and made an extra copy of everything just to be on the safe side. That done, she turned the computer off, made sure all the windows and doors were locked and went to bed.

Despite her exhaustion, sleep didn't come easily. She lay awake for some time, starting at every sound and imagining that she was smelling smoke. Longing for Fletcher welled up in her. She wished he was there just so she could hear the sound of his voice. For a moment, she thought of calling him but it was so late, she'd be bound to wake him.

Reluctantly she settled down in the bed, trying to get comfortable. After a while, it seemed to work. Or perhaps she was so tired it didn't make any difference. She drifted off to sleep.

Her dreams were troubled. She saw fractured images of the fire, Fletcher bare-chested in the flame's glow, holding her afterward, the two of them together on the beach, and in bed. Her dreams had always been vivid, but never quite like this. She caught snatches of sounds—voices, some of them recognizable, others not—bits of music, laughter, all floating by. There were even smells—the garden with its rich earth, the pantry with the perfume of dry herbs, bread baking and smoke but the safe, cheerful kind, confined to a fireplace.

And the sea. Above all, she sensed the sea—smelled and heard it, saw it glimmering under the moonlight in her dreams, turned from it to look back at the house and felt the sense of pride and belonging surge through her.

In her sleep, she smiled. But that faded as the dreams turned darker. Charlotte's face floated by, angry, shouting something at her, blaming her. Gramma Liz was suddenly there, kneeling in the garden, trying to show her something. And a woman she didn't know—beautiful, wise-eyed, with a very serious look on her face, beckoning to her.

Then there were other women, so many of them, calling to her. She could hear their voices, smell the fragrance of their clothes, see their faces, some very like her own. All of them trying to tell her something.

The image faded. She was left alone in a vast space that seemed to have no form. Floating, helpless, she began to struggle. Alarm filled her. She felt the keen edge of panic and opened her mouth to call out.

Abruptly she awoke. Her heart hammered against her ribs and her breathing was labored. She sat up in the bed, clutching the covers to her, and looked around. Part of her almost expected to see the images of her dream, but she was alone. There was nothing but the big, quiet bedroom and the curtains moving gently in the breeze.

Nothing at all.

Yet the remnants of the dream clung to her like sharp, jagged edges. She felt a terrible sense of urgency and dread. Slowly she got out of the bed. She had no real idea of what to do, but the thought of trying to go back to sleep was intolerable. Besides, she was thirsty.

Silently she padded down the hallway to the bathroom. Standing at the sink, she filled a cup with water and drank it. For several seconds, she stared at herself in the mirror as though that might provide a clue as to what was going on in her mind. It didn't.

The heavy sense of unhappiness and apprehension lingered, weighing her down. She decided she'd had all the sleep she was going to get that night.

Perhaps it was just as well. She could use the time to prepare what she had to say to Hobart—and ultimately to Marsdon. She supposed even more of the firm's senior partners would be involved once she announced her findings. They would rake her over the coals to be sure she was right.

There was a lot of pressure these days to leave no stone unturned in examining an audit client. But Kincaid was still an enormously powerful presence in the business world. No one would be eager to go up against him without ample proof of wrongdoing.

Nora was sure she had it, but it wouldn't be a bad idea to go over everything again step by step to make absolutely sure there were no holes. She was just about to start downstairs when a sudden sound made her stop. Frozen on the landing, she listened.

There it was again, faint but unmistakable. The sound of a door opening.

Please, God, let it be the wind. Except she'd closed all the windows. All right then, she told herself, the old house is settling. Except it wasn't. She knew that right down to the bone and sinew of her being. There was a new presence, a sense of the very essence of the house disturbed.

Someone was there.

Her hand went to her throat. Terror threatened to overwhelm her. Quickly she backed away from the stairs, but then stopped. Where could she go?

Whoever it was might start up at any moment. If they were there to do her harm, her bedroom would be the obvious place to look. She had to find somewhere else.

She began backtracking down the hall toward the bathroom. Before she got more than a few yards, she heard the unmistakable tread of a foot on the stairs.

A scream rose in her. She bit it back and pressed herself against the wall, trying to blend in with the shadows there. A shape moved up the steps and paused on the landing. It was very dark but unmistakable—the shape of a man dressed all in black. He even had some sort of covering pulled down over his head and face. But a man all the same.

He hesitated, looking up and down the hall. Nora pressed her lips together. The rush of blood in her ears was so loud she thought he must surely hear it. But after a moment, he turned in the opposite direction, toward the bedroom.

She took a breath and tried to gauge whether she had time to get to the stairs. If she could make it, she could get out of the house. Once outside, she could lose herself in the surrounding woods.

But if he caught her—

She had a split second to make the decision. There was no time for reason. Only instinct could save her and that was telling her not to try it. The house would shelter her. All she had to do was find a place to hide.

Blindly, without thought, she turned. In the days she'd been in the house, she'd done some exploring, but not as much as she would have liked. Work and other—far more pleasurable—things had kept distracting her.

But she knew there had to be an attic. She'd seen it from the outside. All she had to do was find a way to reach it.

The way turned out to be a small, nondescript door set in a far corner of the hallway. It gave way to a narrow, winding staircase that led upward.

Nora shut the door behind her, thankful that it didn't squeak, and crept up the stairs. The air felt cooler and damper than it had below. She realized this level of the house must have never been heated.

At the top of the stairs there was darkness lit only by a round window set at the far end of the attic. Keeping one hand on the wall, she forced herself to keep going. Below, she could hear the intruder come out of the bedroom and start back down the hall, the same way she had gone.

Her throat was so tight that she could barely breathe. She prayed he would think she'd gone downstairs, but the sound got closer, coming past the landing. He was walking down the hall.

She heard a door open, then another. He was checking the other rooms, searching for her. It was only a matter of time—and very little at that—before he found the attic stairs.

Nora ran for the window. She tried to keep her steps as light as possible but speed was essential. If she could get it open and climb out, she might be able to make her way along the roof. But the window had been nailed shut, probably to keep animals from getting in. Try though she did, Nora couldn't budge it.

The steps were near the bottom of the attic stairs. Any second—

The door opened. She saw the faint light from the hall and, most frightening of all, heard a hard laugh.

Kincaid! He'd come himself. But then that made sense considering that both the break-in and the fire had been botched. But how had he known? Why hadn't her ruse worked?

There was no time to think about it. He was coming up the stairs. There was no way out of the attic.

She could try to hide behind the various boxes and trunks that were scattered around, but they would offer her scant protection. Distantly she thought that such an old house should have a far more cluttered attic. What a shame that her ancestors had been so damnably tidy.

What a desperate, dangerous shame.

All the same, she had to try. Crouching behind one of the larger trunks, she held her breath. Kincaid was almost at the top of the steps. He stopped, a big man in excellent condition, and looked around.

Softly he said, "I know you're up here, Nora."

The sound of his voice—so quiet and reasonable with that note of pleasure about it—filled her with horror. They might have been meeting on the street or at a party, so perfectly ordinary did he seem.

"Come on now," he said coaxingly. "I just want to talk. You're a very clever girl, not to mention a highly attractive one. We can work out an arrangement we'll both enjoy."

Nora's stomach twisted. The thought that he actually found her attractive made it all that much worse, and further increased her fear. Slowly, inch by inch, she began trying to move past the attic steps to the distant end of the attic. She had no clear thought in mind except to get away from him.

Kincaid reached the top of the steps, but didn't go any farther. She realized he was giving himself time to adjust to the greater darkness of the attic.

Nora got down on the floor. She could smell the dry scent of ancient wood mingling with the aroma of the herbs that had once dried above it. Slowly, painstakingly, she began crawling.

"This is all so unnecessary," Kincaid said. "I'll admit I've been a bit clumsy, but surely you won't hold that against me? I admire you tremendously. You've done what no one else has been able to."

She could see the far wall, almost touch it. It seemed to draw her irresistibly, yet there was nothing there to help her. Once she reached it, she would be just as trapped as she was now. Perhaps more so.

Still, she couldn't stay where she was. Sooner or later, Kincaid would get tired of listening to his own voice. At least the shadows at the end were deeper. Perhaps she could curl up within them and disappear.

"I've never met a woman like you," Kincaid was saying. The direction of his voice indicated he was moving away from the stairs, straight toward her. "It was a mistake not to acknowledge that. We can make a great pair."

A wave of sickness washed over her. His tone had turned wheedling, but with an underlying note of annoyance. This was all taking too long. He wanted it over with.

Abruptly Nora came to a decision. She couldn't hide and she couldn't run. There was nothing left to do but fight. And for that, she had only one real weapon—her wits.

She had reached the far wall of the attic over the oldest part of the house. There was nowhere left to go. She took a deep breath and got to her feet. From the darkness, she said quietly, "Stay where you are, Robert."

The use of his first name had been deliberate. She saw him stiffen, but he stopped moving, listening intently. Quietly she said, "I've got a gun, but I have no intention of using it if we can talk reasonably."

She did not have a gun. She had never had one. But at that moment, hearing herself speak, she almost believed what she was saying was true. Certainly Kincaid seemed to consider that possibility. He started to take a step forward, but froze.

"All right," he said cautiously. "Throw the gun to me and we'll talk."

Nora laughed. The ease with which she did it astonished her. She'd never considered herself much of an actress before. Obviously being faced with imminent death was bringing out unsuspected talents.

"We'll talk first. How did you know I hadn't gotten your message after the fire?"

"You mean that line you fed Marsdon? Come on, was I really supposed to fall for that?"

"It was more than a line. I flat out lied and said the audit was clean. What tipped you off?"

Kincaid hesitated. Clearly, he preferred her to think he'd seen through her scheme by virtue of his own brilliance. "You went back on the mainframe," he said finally, "to download the files you'd missed."

"And you were watching?"

"That's right, I was. You know, I didn't pay much attention to computers when they started coming in. There were plenty of people around to take care of that for me. But lately I've begun noticing that they're really useful." He chuckled. "Hell, with the right commands, you can find out anything."

"Congratulations," she said. "I thought I'd be safe, but you outsmarted me." Give the man his due, he'd done exactly that. And now she was going to die for it unless she got very lucky, very fast.

"I meant what I said," Kincaid insisted. "You're a remarkable woman. You've got nothing to fear from me. Put down the gun."

"Not yet. Let's go downstairs to talk. You first."

If she could get him onto the first floor, she'd have a chance. But Kincaid wasn't budging.

"Come on," he said, the hard edge creeping back. "I've got to know I can trust you. At least step out where I can see you better."

If she did that, he'd know she wasn't armed. Nora stayed where she was. They were stalemated, but that wouldn't last. He didn't have the patience for it.

"I'll give you the gun downstairs. We can sit and talk, come to an arrangement. To tell you the truth, the thought of being part of your life is tremendously exciting to me."

Actually it made her want to throw up. She thought of Fletcher and blinked back tears.

"I'm beginning to think there is no gun," Kincaid said. He took a step closer.

"Don't."

"In fact, I'm starting to think you're still playing games. After all, you seemed damn excited by that Fletcher guy."

"Who?"

He laughed. "Cute. I saw the two of you at my party and afterward, you wouldn't go out with me. You said it was because of the audit, but I didn't believe that. You were shacking up with him, weren't you? He was here last night. I'll bet the two of you have a real hot thing going."

Nora swallowed the bile that burned her throat. "Stay where you are."

"I don't think so. Come on, honey. It's over. We're just going to have a nice little talk. Nobody's going to get hurt. I'm a rich man, I can pay you whatever you need—"

"No, you aren't."

He stopped, sufficiently startled to be thrown just slightly off balance. "What's that?"

"You heard me. The whole thing's a con. Kincaid Industries is an empty shell. It would have gone bust years ago except you've managed to keep money moving around, making it look as though there was a whole lot more of it than there really was."

"You're crazy. I've got billions."

"You *had* billions. But you made some of the worst real estate deals I've ever seen, not to mention paying top dollar for companies that were going under. What was the problem, Kincaid? Your ego convince you that you could make any deal work? You've got to know it's only a matter of time—and not much of that—before the whole thing just implodes."

"No, it isn't," he shouted. "Nobody else knows. Nobody! I've hidden it too well. What do you think, that I'm stupid? I created an organization that's impenetrable. Nobody could dig deep enough to find out the truth. Nobody but you." The last words were bitten out, heavy with hatred and the promise of violence.

"Not just me," Nora said. She was astonished by how calm she felt. She'd fight him, of course. She might even have some small chance. But the odds were heavily against her. There was an excellent chance that she wasn't going to survive the next few minutes."

"Any halfway decent auditor could have done it," she said. "The next one will and the next one after that. You can't kill us all."

"I won't have to," Kincaid said. "There's money to be had, plenty of it. Drug dealers, terrorists, corrupt governments, they're all looking for places to park cash. I just should have taken it sooner, but I will now. I'll close all the gaps. There'll be nothing for anyone to find."

"How long do you think you'll get along with your new partners?" Nora asked. "They're not likely to tolerate any more mistakes."

"I won't make any more!" Kincaid shouted. "I'm smarter than everyone else, I'm better. That's why I got where I am. You're not going to stop me, you little bitch. I could have given you everything, but you didn't want it. Now I'll give you this—" Metal flashed in the darkness. Kincaid had drawn a long, lethal knife from beneath his sweater. He advanced toward her.

The darkness moved. It welled up suddenly in a surging rush. Nora opened her mouth to scream, thinking she was going to die. Her hands went up instinctively to shield her throat. She kicked out, catching Kincaid in the leg.

Someone shouted—a man. Kincaid. He was shouting something she couldn't make out. Damn... bastard... kill...

Darkness was moving all around her, and a great whirling sound like the wind off the sea overwhelmed her. She crouched down, pressing into the wall, and felt the strength of the old house surge through her. Flickers of the dream returned, the faces of the women, the sense of overflowing pride and power.

She looked up. Two shapes moved in the darkness, struggling. The knife flashed.

Nora leapt. She grabbed for the blade even as it arched downward. There was a single, rending scream, then blood everywhere.

Epilogue

"Better?" Fletcher asked. He wrapped the big bath sheet more securely around Nora. Water dripped down her legs onto the Oriental carpet of the bathroom, but neither of them noticed.

It was very late. The police had come and gone. So had the ambulance. Kincaid had been alive when he reached the hospital, but there wasn't a great deal of hope that he would survive. The blow he'd meant for Fletcher had been deflected by Nora, straight into his own chest.

If he did live, he would never see the outside of a prison again. His own words, thoughtfully caught by Fletcher on the same little video camera he used to record the owls, would prove compelling evidence.

"I can't believe you were there all the time," Nora said. She was trying very hard to be angry, but the sheer joy of being with him, having him there safe with her, overwhelmed all else.

"Not all," he corrected as he took a smaller towel and began drying her hair gently. "I had a clear view of the house from the blind. As soon as he entered, I knew, but it took me a few minutes to realize you were in the attic."

"Thank God, you did," Nora said fervently. She wasn't really so foolish as to wish he'd respected her wish to be left alone. "If you hadn't—"

Fletcher's arms tightened around her. "Don't think about it. It's over."

His body moved against her own. Instantly the familiar heat and longing rose within her. Around them the old house felt once again serene. The images of the dream were gone, but the memory of them lingered.

Nora smiled. All those women—and all those marvelous men. Her family, her heritage. She was a part of it, truly and forever.

"No," she said softly as she raised her mouth to his. "It isn't over. It's only begun."

* * * * *

Get Ready to be Swept Away by
Silhouette's Spring Collection

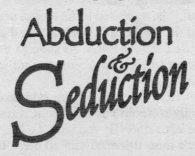

Abduction & Seduction

These passion-filled stories explore both the dangerous
desires of men and the seductive powers of women.
Written by three of our most celebrated authors, they are
sure to capture your hearts.

Diana Palmer
Brings us a spin-off of her Long, Tall Texans series

Joan Johnston
Crafts a beguiling Western romance

Rebecca Brandewyne
New York Times bestselling author
makes a smashing contemporary debut

Available in March at your favorite retail outlet.

Take 4 bestselling love stories FREE

Plus get a FREE surprise gift!

Experience the dark side of love in Silhouette's newest romance series

In January, enjoy these Silhouette Shadows titles:

SS #47 TWILIGHT ILLUSIONS
by Maggie Shayne
Wings in the Night

The empty heart of centuries-old vampire Damien opens up to loving and longing again when mortal Shannon Mallory dares to enter his darkness. Her fatal flaw. Because now Shannon's days are *surely* numbered....

SS #48 DARK OBSESSION
by Amanda Stevens

How can Nick Slade tell Erin Ramsey that her late sister somehow invited the kiss of her killer? And how can he stop the same dark obsession from consuming the woman he would willingly die for?

Don't miss these chilling, thrilling love stories...from Silhouette Shadows.

Available in January at a store near you.

▼ Silhouette® ...where passion lives.

ETERNAL LOVE
by Maggie Shayne

Fans of Maggie Shayne's bestselling Wings in the Night miniseries have heard the whispers about the one known as Damien. And now the most feared and revered of his kind has his own story in TWILIGHT ILLUSIONS (SS #47), the latest in this darkly romantic, sensual series.

As he risks everything for a mortal woman, characters from the previous books risk their very existence to help. For they know the secrets of eternal life—and the hunger for eternal love....

Don't miss TWILIGHT ILLUSIONS by Maggie Shayne, available in January, only from Silhouette Shadows

HE'S A LOVER...
A FIGHTER...
AND A REAL HEARTBREAKER.

Silhouette Intimate Moments is proud to introduce a new lineup of sensational heroes called **HEARTBREAKERS**—real heavyweights in matters of the heart. They're headstrong, hot-blooded and true heartthrobs. Starting in April 1995, we'll be presenting one HEARTBREAKER each month from some of our hottest authors:

> Nora Roberts
> Dallas Schulze
> Linda Turner—and many more....

So prepare yourselves for these heart-pounding HEARTBREAKERS, coming your way in April 1995—only in